Akara Ogun
The Brave Hunter In The Forest of Daemons

Akara Ogun
The Brave Hunter In The Forest of Daemons

A Translation of D. O. Fagunwa
Ogboju Ode Ninu Igbo Irunmale

Edmund Olu Mabo

Previous publications by Daniel Olorunfemi Fagunwa

Other Translations of Ogboju Ode Ninu Igbo Irumole

The Forest of a Thousand Daemons by Wole Soyinka (London: Nelson, 1968) English

La Foresta Dei Mille Demoni by Mario Biondi (Arnoldo Mondadori Editore, 1985) Italian

La Forêt aux Mille Démons by Louis Camara (NENA, 2015) French

400 İlah Ormanı by Bir Avcının Öyküsü (Altıkırkbeş Yayınları, 2016) Turkish

Igbo Olodumare

The Forest of God by Gabriel A. Ajadí (Ibadan: Agbo Areo Publishers, 1994 {1984}) English

In the Forest of Olodumare by Wole Soyinka (London: Nelson, Ibadan: Evans Brothers Ltd., 2010) English

Other Titles

Ireke Onibudo by Alonge Isaac Oluşọla (Ibadan, Nelson Publishers Ltd., 2019) English

The Mysteries of God by Olu Obafemi (Ibadan, Nelson Publishers Ltd., 2012) English

Adiitu Olodumare (1961)

Irinajo, Apa Kiní & Apa Keji (London: Oxford University Press, 1949) Fagunwa's account of his travels in Britain

Taiwo ati Kehinde co-authored with L.J Lewis (London: Oxford University Press, 1949) Primary School Readers

Alaye fun oluko nipa lílo Iwe "Taiwo ati Kehinde", co-authored with L.J Lewis (London: Oxford University Press, 1949) Teachers' Manual

Itan Oloyin (London: Oxford University Press, 1954) An edited collection of folktales.

Ojo Aṣotan, co-authored with G.L. Lasebikan, published posthumously (London: Heinemann Educational Books Ltd., 1964) Short story

Contents

About the Author

Chief Daniel Orowọle Olorunfemi Fagunwa MBE (1903 – 7 December 1963), popularly known as D. O. Fagunwa, was a Nigerian Yoruba author who pioneered the Yoruba-language novel. Fagunwa's novels draw heavily on folktale traditions and idioms, including many supernatural elements. His heroes are usually Yoruba hunters, who interact with kings, sages, and even gods in their quests. Thematically, his novels also explore the divide between the Christian beliefs of Africa's colonizers and the continent's traditional religions. Fagunwa remains the most widely read Yoruba-language author, and a major influence on such contemporary writers as Amos Tutuola. He also used Greek myths and Shakespearean stories as themes in his books, such as in his book *Igbo Olodumare*, where the character Baba-onirugbon-yeuke tells a story similar to Romeo and Juliet. D. O. Fagunwa was the first Nigerian writer to employ folk philosophy in telling his stories. Fagunwa was awarded the Margaret Wrong Prize in 1955 and was made a Member of the Order of the British Empire in 1959.

Daniel Orowole Fagunwa was born in Oke-Igbo, Ondo State in 1903, to Joshua Akintunde Fagunwa and Rachel Osunyọmi Fagunwa. He had three sisters, Mary Adeyemí, Ojuolape and Omotunde. Fagunwa's parents were originally adherents of the traditional Yoruba religion until they converted to Christianity in the late 1910s to early 1920s. He was born with the name Orowole, referring to the Yoruba bullroarer god, Oro. When his family converted to Christianity, he changed his name to Olorunfemi (God loves me). He attended St. Luke's School, Oke-Igbo from 1916 to 1924 and taught as a student teacher there in 1925. After completing his teachers training at St Andrews College in 1929 at Ovo, he taught at various educational establishments from 1930 to 1954. He was Education Officer with the Ministry of Education in Western Nigeria from 1955-59. He married Modakeke in 1937 and in 1938 entered a literary contest of the Nigerian Education Ministry with *Ogboju Ode Ninu Igbo*, widely considered the first novel written in the Yoruba language and one of the first to be written in any African language. Wole Soyinka translated the book into English in 1968 as *The Forest of A Thousand Demons*, first published by Thomas Nelson, then Random House in 1982 and again by City Lights in September 2013. Fagunwa's later works include *Igbo Olodumare* (*The Forest of God*, 1949), *Ireke Onibudo* (1949), *Irinkerindo Ninu Igbo Elegbeje* (*Expedition to the Mount of Thought*, 1954), and *Adiitu Olodumare* (1961).

Daniel Olorunfemi Fagunwa

Translator's Note

I have undertaken the translation of the work of Chief Daniel Orowole Olorunfẹmi Fagunwa, MBE, because he was a man of exemplary talent. As a writer and teacher, he aroused in the minds of his readers a new interest in, and conception of, Nigerian culture in general and that of the Yoruba tribe in particular. His books are works of creative genius, written not only to tell a story but to illustrate the social habits of the time in terms of a moral doctrine. Fagunwa intention is to make his readers conscious of themselves as individuals and of their responsibilities towards one another, nature and God. At many points throughout his books, he seeks to expose the reality underlying human life, in which man is conceived as a potential force, capable of shaping his own destiny.

To this end Fagunwa was fond of using long, repetitive phrases to illustrate the various meanings of his stories, but in many cases his extremely picturesque imagery is such that to attempt to translate them literally would result in impenetrable obscurity. To resolve this, I have looked for simple, and not too rigorous, English equivalents, which express the idea without sacrificing the picturesque, poetic style which is dominant in most of his work. In translating, I have not only aimed to simplify the construction of often complex ideas, but to help the reader to grasp their meaning and to follow the stories. But ultimately, the question of how much of the story is conveyed by means of this translation, and how effectively, must be left for the judgement of the individual reader.

E. O. Mabo

CHAPTER 1

Akara-Ogun and his Parents

When music is played, my dear friends, it follows the notation of music; but only those who appreciate the sound of music can respond to it, and of them, only the enlightened can understand it. The story that follows is like music. I will play it to you, and you, O wise ones who appreciate the sound of such music, will respond to it – and being enlightened, will understand it.

I remind you that if someone is endowed with an extraordinary talent, one should not hesitate to declare it, for I don't want a half-hearted or half-interested response. I want you to respond to it seriously, with your minds fully engaged; thus you will gain the respect of your fellows, reflecting the high quality of the story itself. But if you are really to enjoy this story, you must do two things for yourself. You must place yourself in the story, imagining that you are one of the characters; thus, you will respond to what you hear as a participant. Secondly, as a person of enlightenment, you will need to understand the meaning of the story as it unfolds.

But I do not want to say too much about that at this stage, lest I seem to stray from the point – I will take up my metaphorical instrument and start to play, asking only that you make yourself comfortable, ready to listen attentively. Thus my act of communication and yours of listening will complement each other, just as if you were to provide the music while I dance – one good turn deserves another!

The story I am about to narrate, started one beautiful morning when the weather was clear and bright; the wild animals were still asleep, the domestic animals were already foraging and the birds were trumpeting their songs of praise. The breeze was blowing over green vegetation, the sun was shining in glorious splendour and people were getting on with their daily routines. I settled down comfortably in my chair to enjoy the morning. Presently an old man came up and greeted me. I responded, and offered him the chair opposite. Once he was settled we started chatting and laughing as if we had known each other for ages, but just as the mood was established he sighed, as if he was thinking of something serious. Before I could ask what was troubling him, he began to speak.

"Please get out your writing materials, and set down the story that I am about to tell you. Don't put it off for another day, lest you lose the opportunity. I only come here today because I have been thinking about the future; I fear that I may die unexpectedly, and my story will die with me. But if you record it carefully as I dictate it now, it will never be forgotten, even after I am long dead."

I brought out my materials as soon as he had finished speaking, drew up my chair and once I was comfortable

I told him I was ready to listen. He began to dictate, as follows.

My name is Akara-Ogun, which has a similar meaning to Nimrod in your Bible, for I was one of the ancient brave hunters. My father was a hunter and healer, what you would call a medicine-man or witch doctor. He had a great collection of magical objects, including oracular woodcarvings which he used for divination, and he knew many spells and charms. Whenever he was away from home his house was guarded by genies, so that no one dared enter, not even the bravest. Yet, despite his expertise with the supernatural, he had no great influence over my mother, who was a witch of great power.

At one time my father had three other wives, and sired nine children, but my mother was his senior wife, and I was the eldest of her four children. His second wife had three and his third two, but his fourth wife had none.

One day a quarrel arose between my mother and one of the other wives, and they brought it to my father for settlement. Unfortunately, as it turned out, he judged in favour of the junior wife. My mother was greatly offended, and decided to exact a desperate revenge, using her skill in witchcraft. As a result, within a year all eight of my brothers and sisters were dead, along with the other three wives. I was thus the only child, and my mother the only wife.

Please take note of this, my dear friend, and if you are not yet married, think carefully before you do! Of course your wife should be beautiful and attractive otherwise you will soon get bored with each other. But that should not be the only consideration; it is just as important that your wife should be intelligent if you are to live in harmony, but even that is not of the first importance. Above all, you must look for a wife who is of, at least reasonably, good character, since she will hold the key to your life's secrets. You must remember that, because women are so close to men, they can and will use any means at their command to secure whatever they want, and there is no way that we can avoid their influence. What I have to tell you of my father's experiences will give you pause.

It happened one day when my father decided to go hunting in the forest. After a few hours he was tired, and decided to rest a while on a fallen tree. Soon after he settled down he noticed that the ground in front of him was starting to crack. A plume of smoke poured out, engulfing the surroundings, so that he could hardly see – everywhere was completely dark. As he was trying to find his way out, the smoke gathered into a spiral column, which presently solidified into a muscular man carrying a sword. He walked towards my father, who turned and ran, but the man demanded that he stop, caught up with him and addressed him as follows.

"Can you not see that I am no mere mortal? I am newly arrived from Heaven, and I am sent here specifically to kill you. Run where you like, I shall kill you for sure!"

My father was terrified, but he called up his courage and replied, "I can see that you are from Heaven, and that your sword is meant to harm me. Nevertheless, I entreat you, for God's sake! Tell me, how have I offended?"

The Man replied, "Didn't you know that it would offend your God, when you destroyed his creation? Have you not brought the lives of eleven people to a sudden end?"

This accusation greatly surprised my father, because, despite his mastery of supernatural power, he had never misused it to do harm. He therefore replied, "If that is why you are here, your mission is justified. But you have got the wrong man – it was surely not I, for never since I was born have I harmed anybody; I have never borne a grudge against anyone for any reason, nor coveted their possessions. Moreover, I have never caused anyone injury, nor have I aimed my gun at anyone. Why, therefore, should you kill me for what I have never done?"

The Man replied, "It is true that you have never directly killed anybody, but you are nonetheless guilty of causing the innocent to suffer. You knowingly married a malevolent witch for the sake of her beauty. Was that a responsible action? Are you not even now being haunted by the ghosts of three wives? Are you not to blame for the deaths of eight children? Yet despite all this, do you now have the effrontery to tell me you have done no wrong? I should surely kill you!"

It was only then that my father realized what sort of woman he was married to. He replied, saying, "Indeed, now I can see my fault. I have married a woman over whom I cannot exercise the control of a responsible husband. I have left undone those things which I ought to have done, as the Christians say. I have taken a wrong course, and have sung the praises of one whom I should have got rid of. Alas! Man of Heaven, please forgive me!"

When he heard this the Man forgave my father, and spared his life, but only on condition that he should kill my mother as soon as he got home. Having issued this warning, he disappeared into the forest. As soon as he was gone my father picked up his gun and set off home, taking a route that led through a field of okra. By the time he got to his own farm it was already getting dark, but the early evening moon was bright. When he got to the boundary of his own farm, and looked across it, he saw someone approaching from the opposite direction. He quickly climbed a tree to see what that person would do. The person approached a big anthill, and walked inside it. After a little while a deer came out of the ant-hill and went to feed on the okra. My father took aim and shot the deer in its head. As the shot went home, the deer bellowed in a human voice, "I am injured!"

My father dropped out of the tree, and ran to a little shed on the okra farm, where he spent the night. At daybreak he went back to where he had shot the deer, but found nothing except a blood-trail leading away. He followed it, but lost it in the town centre. He set off home, and was surprised to find it again, leading right to his own doorstep, and from there to my mother's bedroom.

I should mention at this point that I had not slept at home that night, because I always kept away from the house when my father was absent, so as to avoid the guardian genies, who were uncomfortable company. My mother, too, rarely slept at home on such occasions, except with the approval of my father. However, I got back just as my father was about to open the door to my mother's room, so we went in together. I almost bolted in terror when I saw my mother, for she looked like a centaur. She had the head and shoulders of a human being, but the body and legs of a deer. There was blood all over her, and swarms of flies buzzed round her body. When my father touched her he found she was already dead and starting to decompose. He had never known that my mother used to transform herself into a deer and sneak out at night to eat the okra.

Thus did my mother die, but her malice survived, for my father died barely a month later, leaving me an orphan. So, with the end of my parents' story, mine begins. Well done, my friend.

Akara-Ogun,
the brave hunter

CHAPTER 2

The Experiences of Akara-Ogun on his First Visit to the Forest of Daemons

That adventure of my father's was as nothing compared with mine, and when I think about it, I feel quite terrified of what those who are older than I am must go through. If the elderly have to recount their life-experiences, some youths would rather die before they reach old age.

I was ten years old when I began to accompany my father on hunting expeditions, and had my own gun by the time I was fifteen. My father died ten years after that, so naturally I inherited his wealth and his magical practice. Long before he died I had killed elephant and buffalo, as well as many other kinds of animal, with my own gun.

It was one afternoon three months after my twenty-sixth birthday that I picked up my gun and set out to hunt in the great Irunmale Forest, which is also called the Forest of Daemons, about six hours' walk from our home town of Oke-Igbo, which means in our language, Forest Hill. The way through the forest goes on to Mount Langbodo and from there to Heaven. The forest itself is full of all manner of wonderful things, including many dangerous animals and mysterious birds. It is not only they who make it the most dangerous of forests, for elves are to be found there also.

It took me a long time to reach the forest, and it was getting so dark that I could hardly see a thing. I was so tired by then that I couldn't even light my lamp to hunt by, so I made a fire in a hollow in the body of a tree and roasted and ate a piece of yam that I had brought with me. Thereafter I gathered fallen leaves for my bed and lay down, with my hunting bag for a pillow and my gun fully loaded beside me. Soon after I had gone to sleep I was woken by the noise of the elves who were trading by night as is their custom.

It is not generally known that, although the creatures are active by day as well, they prefer to work at night. It is also during the night that they hold consultations with their King, whose title is Olori-igbo, which means King of the Forest. I was unhappy to discover that the tree where I had built my fire was supposed to be the palace of the king. I was naturally frightened, so I picked up my bag and gun and carefully climbed up one branch of the tree. I got to the top without realizing that I was actually climbing the head of the King himself! This made my offence the greater, since my action was perceived as trespass.

After I had been some time at the top of the tree the elven chiefs began to arrive. They built a massive fire to one side, which illuminated the tree, and they sat round it. They were of many different kinds, and I had a panoramic view. Some walked on their heads, some hopped about like frogs and others had neither arms nor legs, and rolled like barrels. The King's minstrel was the last to arrive, and immediately began a chant.

"King of the Forest! King of the Forest! You are the guardian of the elves. I repeat, you are the guardian of the elves, and there is no guardian like you! As your meals consist of various parts of the human body, such as the arms, breast and skull, what can any human being do to you, King of the Forest? Are you walking on your head? If I may ask again, are you walking on your head? I ask this because I can see your eyes are upside-down, glowing with anxiety. King of the Forest, are you feeling unwell? Why don't you come out? We are all waiting for you."

After he had finished, the King raised his voice in reply, so loud that it reverberated through the entire forest. The wild animals were frozen in fright, the birds sleeping in their nests were woken, the fish dived to the bottom and even the wild vegetation bent to the sheer volume of his voice. Nothing moved, and all in the forest were silent as the King bellowed: "Eeeeh! Eeeeh! the fire burning below is caused by a human being, therefore the King of the Forest cannot come out today. Have you not noticed the object dangling above?"

Elven chief with remains
of their King's last meal

When he had finished, they all looked up and saw me. Ah! How they started dancing and rejoicing, as they planned to kill and eat me. But while they were wandering how to get me down, I remembered one of my magical spells which could make me invisible. I immediately invoked its power with an incantation, and found myself back in my own home.

After I had rested a while I felt ashamed, and said to myself, "Is this not a great disgrace? I claim to be a hunter, yet I was humiliated and forced back from the very first hunting trip I made after my father's death. It is more honourable to die than to be humiliated in this way. To prove that I am still worthy to be called Akara-Ogun, I must go back to the same forest. I shall defeat any witch or wizard who threatens my life, and any elf who dares to tempt me or to discount my power, shall suffer the consequences. That which goes up shall surely come down! So let the Almighty God ensure my safe return."

Having thus fortified myself, I recited an incantation that would take me back to the forest. The response was immediate, but instead of finding myself on the King of Elf Tree, I was on top of a palm tree together with my gun. The spikes made it painful to move about, and I had not been there long when it started to rain. It kept on raining throughout the night, but when it stopped I came down, got out my matches (which I kept safe from the damp in an oiled wrapper), and made myself a little bonfire at the base of the tree.

Once the fire was going, I took off my jumper to dry in front of it, and as soon as it was dry I took off my trousers to dry as well. Then I roasted and ate a piece of yam. After I had finished eating, I took out my pipe and soon got it going. Once the smoke was copiously pouring forth, I was quite content.

As I was puffing away enjoyably, I heard someone grousing from a nearby walnut tree. When I turned to look I saw a fat, dark man who was grumbling, "Those stinkers have brought their nuisance here again."

I ignored him and kept on puffing because I recognized him as a walnut goblin and the smell of tobacco was irritating to him. Goblins hate aromatic smells, especially tobacco. But he grumbled still more, so I turned in his direction and puffed out a plume of tobacco smoke, which so greatly offended him that he belched further abuse at me: "You're a dirty idiot with no sense of bodily hygiene, whose stench causes annoyance to everyone!" This made me very angry, so I turned towards him and replied, "How dare you speak to me so rudely? You're a horrible filthy stinker yourself, and if you don't behave better I shall have to burn you down." When he heard my warning, he quietened down and walked off, hissing in annoyance.

Although it had rained all night, to my surprise the sun shone brightly from dawn onwards, and continued throughout the day. At about breakfast time I picked up my gun, strapped my hunting bag across my shoulder, and went into the forest to look for game. I wandered about for a while, but didn't come across a single animal to shoot at, though I heard birdsong in the distance. I didn't realize that I was still far from the best areas for animals, but I was delighted when I got there, and sat down to get my gun ready. Then I plucked some leaves to camouflage myself and waited by a tree to watch the animals.

When finally I had the opportunity to start shooting, I suddenly noticed a strange little creature about the height of my hip, carrying a small mat and grumbling to himself. As he did so, tears poured down his cheeks and his nose was running as well. For a while I thought he would stop, but instead his lamentations intensified. He wept and screamed continually and the intensity of this behaviour frightened the animals away. After a while I found I could no longer tolerate such a nuisance. "Why do all you elves behave so shamelessly and repulsively?" I demanded. "What exactly are you crying for? Why are you carrying that mat? If you don't quieten down at once, I shall certainly shoot you dead." On hearing that he gave me a look of contemptuous disgust before replying. "How typical of human beings: ungrateful creatures that you are! We have long seen how restless you are, and how insatiable in your greed and ambition. Those who prosper among you always look for the maximum prestige and gratification that you can obtain, forgetting that you are not born equal and scorning those of lesser capacity. It is also in your nature that your minds are never at peace. Those who are happy today may bring grief to themselves and their families tomorrow. "Apart from that, you humans are preoccupied with various problems – death one moment, disease the next; a quarrel today, discomfort tomorrow; grief this week, sadness next. Therefore, when we contemplate the experiences you go through, we feel sorry for you; we lament for you, which make our noses run, but does it win us your affection? No! Do you even welcome us when we meet? That neither! Instead you despise us for carrying our mats about, and for our runny noses, you regard our concern as a punishment for some mysterious sin, and you have stigmatized us with the scornful name of 'The Weeping Goblins'."

To be honest, I felt a little ashamed at what the creature said, because his account of human behaviour was true. However, since I didn't want to give the impression that I was offended or abashed by his frank remarks, I laughed apologetically, and said I was only joking. Having accepted this he resumed his weeping and went on his way. He had only gone a short distance when I remembered the adage of my people that, 'every man is the author of his own destiny', and asked myself why I should not take advantage of this golden opportunity to ask a favour of him. I therefore caught up with him, prostrated myself before him, and implored him to grant me a boon. He seemed very pleased that I had taken his words so much to heart, and presented me with four pods of alligator pepper, two at a time. He instructed me that if ever I was in difficulty, I should break and eat a single pepper seed from one of the first pair. I would then grow wings that would enable me to fly like a bird. Once

I wanted the wings to disappear, I should eat a seed from one of the second pair. I was later to discover that this magical gift was very effective.

He then continued on his way and I went back into the forest to carry on with my hunting. I had only walked a short distance when I saw more animals running about, but as I was looking for a suitable vantage from which to shoot at them, I saw that once again, there was a short man chasing them away. This man was not as tall as the one I had met earlier, and he was very dark. Once again I was very annoyed, and spoke sternly to him. "You elves are a wicked lot with no consideration for others – which doubtless accounts for your lack of height, and why you keep wandering about in this aimless fashion. Here, there are animals in abundance, but not only do you have no interest in hunting them yourselves, you spoil the sport for those who do."

After I had finished my tirade he looked me up and down contemptuously, hissed and replied. "I am the Crown Prince of the Forests [Alade-Igbo], the goblin who lives inside an anthill. If you don't know me, you should at least have heard of me! Either way you should treat me with respect. Everyone knows better than to be rude in my presence, and you are lucky that I happen to be in a good mood today; otherwise I might have brought home to you what it means to go hunting in Irunmale Forest, which is rightly called the Forest of Daemons. I may be small in size, but I lack none of the useful qualities – especially intelligence and good sense.

I never attempt anything which is beyond my power, nor do I contemplate that which can never be accomplished. On the contrary, I always think carefully before I act, so that I will have nothing to regret afterwards. I don't transgress my limits, and I have been minding my own business since the day I was born.

"Contrast my way with that of you arrogant human creatures. See how you squander your money, thinking you are buying valuable assets, only to find too late that you have wasted your substance on the superficial pleasures of life. You seek to please your fellows by attempting the impossible, and only after you have failed, do you discover how capriciously difficult to please they are – like yourself. Whoever they have praised today, they will most likely condemn tomorrow or vice versa, for it's all one with you. If one of you plans something ambitious, his fellows will mock him, but if his plan works, they will turn round and praise his vision, and say they believed in it all along. There is no one that they can't carp at; they disparage the poor no less than the rich, the common people as well as the famous, and they even insult their own king, if that's what they feel like doing. Therefore, kindly continue on your journey and I will carry on with mine – minding my own business!" With that he went on his way. I have to say that by now I was thoroughly fed-up with the Forest, because all the elves I had met so far had been rude to me. Nevertheless, after this

had gone, I began to overhear the activities of some animals in the distance. They seemed to be jumping from tree to tree, but when I concentrated my attention in that direction, I discovered that it was only two small monkeys. I shot and killed one and put it in my hunting bag which I now carried on my head, and with my gun hanging over my shoulder, I walked down to my shed by the palm tree.

Once I got there, I made up a fire and put the monkey on it to burn away the fur. Once this was done, I got out my knife and made a small barbecue frame up to about the height of my knee, so that I could roast the animal. Those pieces that were too small to put on the frame I roasted separately, and ate on the spot. The monkey had been young and well fed and tasted delicious.

Shortly after this, night began to fall, and at exactly eight o'clock I lit my hunting lamp, strapped it on my head and went hunting for more animals. Soon I spotted an animal shape at a reasonable distance and shot it dead. I came up to the body and discovered that it was a jackal which I carried back to my shed. There I flayed and jointed it, and roasted it together with the monkey which was already on the flame. I didn't bother to hunt any more that night, but went to sleep as soon as the jackal was finished.

The call of a cuckoo woke me up in the morning, which was my third day hunting in the Forest of Daemons. I breakfasted on cold roast monkey and jackal, loaded my gun, slung my bag over my shoulder and set out after further game. I am sorry to confess that such was my feeling of well-being that I neglected to take with me the many magical charms which I usually regarded as necessary. I left most of them in my shed by the palm tree, and packed nothing extra except some bullets and a cutlass.

I hadn't gone far when I encountered my first animals of the day, but they were completely panic-stricken, running helter-skelter in all directions. When I got a chance to shoot at one, I heard a noise like the footsteps of six heavy men approaching from the distance. I recognized it from the descriptions of many experienced hunters: it was Agbako, whose name means Calamity, the notorious sixteen-eyed freak-monster. I must admit I was absolutely terrified when I saw him. He wore a metal helmet, a jumper made of lead and a pair of leather shorts. Below the knees, his legs were covered with palm leaves while strings of leather charms hung from his navel to his hip. These were full of frightening objects, including a live snake which flicked out its tongue as he walked. He had a big, oblong head, and his sixteen eyes were arranged in a row at jaw-level. No one could look into these eyes without fear, for they revolved continually in a clockwise direction. His hair was bushy, thick, filthy and very long and unkempt. Agbako carried two clubs in his right hand and three sheathed swords in his left. He was well known for his malevolence.

As soon as he saw me, he turned in my direction with evil intent. As he came closer, I conjured up a spell to make him disappear, and indeed, he did vanish into the forest. But he made a counter-response to my spell with the result that I found myself in the forest standing right before him. I was quite terrified and reversed my original spell to take me back to the path. This worked but as I landed, I found myself once again confronted by Agbako. Next I tried a spell to return him to the forest, but this time tied down with twigs. That too worked precisely according to my command, but once again he reciprocated, and I found myself lying in front of him and tied down in the same way. This was terrifying and also very uncomfortable, so I screamed out another conjuration to untie me and take me back to the path; but as soon as I landed there, once again Agbako was before me.

As he was clearly unavoidable, I challenged him to a fight, and in no time we were grappling. We fought for a long time with no sign that either would overcame the other, though we were both drenched with sweat and gasping for breath. My eyes were red with exertion, but he was in no better state, and we had trampled the ground flat and open.

After a long time I was becoming tired, but Agbako showed no sign of it, however he may have been feeling. I tried to disengage, but he kept his grip and I was too tired to break it. But then he realized how tired I was, and released me voluntarily. He took a small gourd from his bag, and tapped it with his forefinger. It turned into a keg of palm wine. He sat down, took out a pair of drinking vessels, and poured a drink which he offered to me. Then he poured one for himself. When we had finished half the keg, and rested long enough to get our breath back, he said that I had had enough and should drink no more. Then he said that we should resume fighting, and so we set to.

After we had been wrestling for a while, I withdrew and retreated to get out my cutlass. While he was still struggling to get his own cutlass out of its sheath I got behind him and stabbed him with all my might in the back of his head; but to my disappointment that had no effect on him at all – far from it, my cutlass snapped halfway down the blade, with the end flying off down the clearing.

Seeing what had happened he recovered the broken end and took the handle from me. Then he laid the two halves against each other, and they melted together, restoring it to a perfect weapon without so much as a hairline crack. After that he demanded that we resume fighting. By now I was so tired that I could hear the pounding of my own heart. Nevertheless, I carried on, and once again stabbed at him with my cutlass, this time in the side. Before I could withdraw he slashed at my wrist, severing hand and cutlass together. I crashed down heavily on my bottom, in deadly pain, but Agbako picked up my hand and rubbed the severed end with his spittle. He did the same to my stump, and when he brought the two together they became whole again, as if I had suffered no damage at all.

He looked at me, burst out laughing, and said it was time to resume the fight. I was even more terrified than before, and wondered how I would ever survive such an ordeal. I screamed out a magical summons: "All creatures of the Forest, and all visitors, please help me!"

Soon every sort of creature that inhabited Irunmale Forest began to arrive. The elves, the animals and the birds all appeared, and assembled in separate groups, but Agbako took no heed of any of them, and pulled me off the ground to continue the fight. Whatever movement I made, and whatever physical action I took, Agbako reciprocated precisely, so it was a fierce fight.

After the elves had watched us wrestling for a while, I saw one of them coming towards where we were fighting. He signalled that Agbako should release me, and Agbako obliged. The elf then offered me a portion of kola nut which I ate. As soon as I had finished, I found my spirit recharged with a new access of immense energy. I threw myself at Agbako and seized him by the neck. I squeezed hard, he bellowed like an animal, and all the elves yelled. But when I tried to lift him so as to smash him into the ground, his feet remained firmly rooted to the spot. He was absolutely immovable, but when he tried to lift one of my legs so that he would be able to kick the other one from under me, I remained in just as firm a contact with the ground. He punched me, but I felt no hurt; he kicked me, but I was unaffected. His entire body was fearfully hot and flushed; his breath was like a raging storm. It made me giddy, and to prove how truly he deserved the name of Agbako he stamped his foot on the ground. It immediately cracked open beneath us, and engulfed us both.

When I got to the bottom, I found myself inside a house, but there was no sign of Agbako. In fact, I never saw him again until the time, long afterwards, when we set out on an expedition to Mount Langbodo. (I will tell you all

The Epic Fight of Akara-Ogun and Agbako

about this later.) Nevertheless, for as long as I live I will never forget what I experienced before I escaped from this underground place – indeed, it will still be fresh in my memory long after I am dead and in Heaven.

The underground house where I found myself was quite small, but its walls and floor had been treated with cow-dung and its ceiling was completely covered with rows of guns. It was quite bright inside, yet it had neither doors nor windows, and I was unable to see any source for the light. As I stood at the centre, I suddenly noticed that the walls were closing in on me from all sides, so that the space got progressively narrower, and I feared that my fate was to be crushed to death. I was petrified, but just as the walls were about to reach my body, they began to retreat to their original positions and the house resumed its former size and shape. Then, when I was beginning to relax, the guns on the ceiling began to fire, so that bullets buzzed about the house and the walls shook so much that I thought I would fall. For a while I managed to remain upright, but I became more and more confused, as the elf had predicted. Ultimately I lost my balance, and fell down on my hands and knees.

When the shooting finally stopped, I realized I was blind. I could feel some people touching me with very cold hands. After a while, I could hear them dancing around me, laughing and clapping their hands over my head and I could clearly hear the loud, quick clatter of their footsteps. This only lasted a short time after which they began to toss me up and catch me repeatedly, like a bouncy ball.

Next they set me down on my feet, stripped off my clothes and dressed me in others which I couldn't see. They never stopped laughing in all this time. At last someone rubbed his hand over my face and I regained my sight, but when I looked around, no one was there. I found myself sitting on a big chair, and my body had changed past recognition for I was fat and covered in feathers. By fat I don't mean fat all over – my arms and legs were the same size as usual, but my stomach was twelve times its former size and my head was sixteen times bigger. Despite that my neck was only a little thicker, it had grown very long. I was greatly amused by my new appearance but decided to remain seated, since I feared that my legs might not support the weight of my stomach. The weight of my head was putting a strain on my neck even when sitting down.

After a while I began to feel hungry, and I was wondering how I could find something to eat when I saw in front of me two portions of corn meal and a dish of meat stew. I tried to reach out for it, but my huge stomach prevented me. I was still straining after it when I noticed that the food was moving slowly towards me. When it came into reach, I took a morsel, but found that while my neck was as long as a crane's, its bone was too stiff and inflexible to bend forward, and my arm wasn't long enough to reach my mouth. It must have been great fun for anyone watching to see my struggles. The funniest part would have been when I tried to push the food in, but only got crumbs and droplets of oil all down my arm and my neck.

Take note, my dear friend, life without food is no life at all. I must say at this point that I am very fond of food, and cannot bear to go hungry. That is why some people call me Akara-Ogun, the Great Gourmand. I actually answer to that nickname, which should explain why I was so desperate to eat at this time. I was still striving to solve that problem when I found a small piece of wood nearby, which I used like a chopstick to put the corn meal in my mouth. Unfortunately the amount it picked up was too large, as despite the new size of my head, my mouth was no larger than before. When I finally got the big lump of corn meal to my lips it blocked the entrance, making it very difficult for me to eat the whole piece at one time. Consequently, as I tried to eat the part of the big lump that was actually in my mouth, hoping to, gradually, reduce its size until I could consume the lot, the big portion which was blocking my mouth fell off my lips. I carried on for a long time, but was quite unable to find a satisfactory way of eating.

I had heard people laughing nearby from the moment I started trying to eat, but I never saw them, and after a while I screamed in rage and frustration, "In the name of God! I appeal to whoever is laughing over there to please change me back to what I was before, if you are those responsible for my present situation. I regret my fight with Agbako, and I promise never to make that mistake again. If at any time in the future I become aware of his presence, I shall do my very best to avoid all contact with him. I therefore appeal to you – please help me!"

Once I had finished, they stopped laughing, and after a while I noticed my stomach had started to reduce, as had my head and neck. Soon my body had returned to its usual proportions, and I heard nothing more from the elves after that. But I was still imprisoned in the same house, and I could still see no way out. Then at what I took to be nightfall, as it was beginning to get dark, one of the walls split down the middle and in walked a beautiful lady, accompanied by a multitude of young girls. They were all so very lovely that I was embarrassed by them, and afraid to make eye-contact; but the lady approached me.

"Akara-Ogun," she said, "You must realize by now that this world is full of all types of mysterious and supernatural characters, including fairies, goblins, elves, gnomes and ghosts. Collectively, they include all the daemonic creatures of this world. I am one of them, and my name is Iranlowo [Help]. I love God and He loves me, and our relationship is good on both sides. He responds to all my supplications, and I am always His obedient servant. Thrice daily, I traverse the world, visiting and bringing help to all the friends of God, according to their degree of devotion to Him. Those who show little love for him get only a little help from me; while those who show him much love receive much help in return. Those who care for Him receive my care as well; those who treat him with disrespect receive no respect from me, for all must reap what they sow. If you make a good investment, you will receive a good return, while those who invest according to bad advice get what they deserve.

However as their circumstances may vary in this world, God shall reward everyone as they should be rewarded. Therefore, Akara-Ogun, I want you to get up and follow me, for you are destined to be an important agent of God."

When she had finished speaking, I got up and followed her out of the house into the forest. From there we went on through valleys and over hills; we crept under trees and waded through swamps. After some time, we came to a crossroads where she stopped to direct me on my way. "Please carry on walking and take note of the things you will encounter in this town. Don't be afraid or nervous, and remember that my name means Help, and that I will never let you down in this world."

I listened attentively and then set off in the direction she had indicated while she went on her own way. Soon I arrived at the town she had mentioned. From the moment I entered until I reached the market square (which was about ten minutes' walk) I noticed how quiet it was, for although I met many people, when I greeted them they responded only by murmuring a few words which I could not understand. In the market I took up a position under a tree from which I watched what there was to see.

It amazed me that the corpses of innumerable children were strewn about the market, but no one was paying them the least attention. Though the stench was ferocious, and flies swarmed all over, nobody thought it necessary to bury them. After I had been standing there a short while, a lady approached and greeted me. I was pleased to see her and responded cordially and then mentioned how astonished I was that no one in the market spoke above a murmur while those I had greeted had made no response.

She looked distressed at this and replied; "My name is Iwapele [Humility], and the name of this town is Emo, which means Trouble. It is a place of ill repute, on account of its decadence and poverty. It is also plagued by greed and hatred, envy and theft, quarrels and arguments, death and disease. It is a town of outlaws, for once long ago the people committed a sin so serious that the sun refused to shine on it for six whole months, and the moon for three years. No rain would fall on it, and all the crops of corn, yam and banana failed. There was no law, only chaos. "Nevertheless, in time God took pity on the people. He knew that it was He who had created them, and therefore He forgave them, but He warned them never to repeat their crime. Thereafter, everything went back to normal, but as soon as they were comfortable again they forgot the words of their Creator. They returned to following their own thoughts and their own desires, but God knew what they were doing, because all deeds and all thoughts are known to God, 'from whom no secrets are hid', as the Christians put it. He therefore sent emissaries to investigate the malpractices of this sinful town.

"They came disguised as human beings, and stayed in my house. I welcomed them cordially, and looked after them as well as my means would allow. They stayed only briefly, but long enough to deliver the message that God had entrusted to them. They struck the people dumb and blind, and laid the town under a perpetual curse from which only I was spared. Therefore, since I happen to meet you today, it is my wish that you should remain here from now on, to live with me in my house and keep me company because only those who share a common interest are compatible. I can see that we are of the same kind so I have no doubt that we will be compatible."

Having heard what she had to say, I told her that I would do exactly as she had suggested for I was tired of wandering aimlessly without direction or design. But first I asked her to spare me a few minutes so that I could see what was going on in the market before we left for her house. It was only now when she had explained matters that I realized all the people were blind and dumb. I had not suspected this because their eyes were all wide open and so I assumed they could see, not realising their eyesight was absent.

I observed a great deal in the market, more than it is possible for me to recount now though I will definitely tell you about them next time. Nevertheless, I will tell you about a few of these things, so that it won't appear that I am trying to avoid the subject completely.

The first notable sight was a severely crippled man who could only hop about on crutches. He passed me in an evident hurry and carried on towards a pond. I shouted a warning that to go in that direction would do him no good, but he ignored me, falling in and getting drenched as a result. I felt sorry for him, but he showed no signs of distress. He emerged laughing from the pond and hopped on his way. He had barely hopped three times when he stumbled into a woman. She was annoyed, and drew back her arm to strike at him, but hit someone else by mistake. He was equally annoyed, and also struck back, but hit a third party. From there it developed into a chain reaction, with everyone in the market attacking each other.

In the confusion, many children fell from their mothers' backs and were trampled underfoot in the struggle, as also happened to those old or infirm people who fell and were unable to get up quickly. Some people who had lost babies tried to rescue them, and often picked up someone else's, or one of the many dead I have mentioned. All these misfortunes befell them because they had displeased God.

I noticed also that many people wore their clothes wrongly. Men wore their jackets back to front or inside out, and some women had their head- ties fastened on the wrong side. Moreover, all their clothes were as dirty as hunter's bags. I saw much else in their market, which I have no time to recount now, and it was enough to make up my mind. Despite our brief acquaintance, I decided to join Iwapele at her house, and we started to live together.

I visited the law court regularly, and noted that sometimes when someone had committed a crime and was to be brought to justice, the police would arrest one of the nobility by mistake. Often this dignified person would have been repeatedly and seriously assaulted by the police before the mistake came to light. Sometimes when the King wanted to go riding, he found his servants had saddled up a bull for him, and so it went on, in confusion and disorientation.

Once I was settled in, Iwapele told me that there was one room in her house which I must never enter during her lifetime, although she said I could do whatever I liked after she was dead when the whole house would become my property. I obeyed her in this, because I loved her greatly; indeed, I was so devoted to her that I was considering a formal proposal of marriage, but just before I did so she fell ill and died, much to my surprise, for I was quite a lot older than she.

This brought me face to face with the reality of death, for no one is too young or too old to die. After the truth of her death sank in I wept bitterly until my eyes were so swollen and sore that I could hardly see. But no amount of tears can bring the dead back to life; it will only do harm to your eyes. However bitter our feelings of grief and loss, they can never influence what has already happened.

After the death of Iwapele I began to think about leaving the town. As I settled down to make my plans I suddenly remembered the room which she had warned me never to enter until after her death. I got up, dressed and decided to find out exactly what it contained. I was naturally frightened as I stood before the door, but when I considered the experience I had gone through in the past I was determined to open it.

I entered the room, but as soon as I was in it, I recognised it for my own room at home and when I looked around

I found the gun which I had dropped in the place where Agbako and I had fought. I also found my hunting bag and everything else which I had lost in Irunmale Forest. In addition, I found in one corner a bag of money with which I bought food and some new clothes.

So ends the story of my first experience in that terrible forest. Perhaps now you will get me something to eat, as I am getting hungry. When I have finished eating I will tell you the story of my second experience, which, I assure you will be far more interesting than this first one.

That was how the man related his first experience during his first visit to Irunmale Forest, rightly called Daemonic! While he rested I prepared some food which we both ate, and as I realized it was getting dark, I suggested that he go home that night and come back next morning. I saw him off and we bade each other goodnight.

CHAPTER 3

The Experiences of Akara-Ogun on his Second Visit to the Forest of Daemons

After Akara-Ogun returned home, I summoned all my neighbours, friends, acquaintances and relatives and recounted what I had heard. They were most amazed and decided to come to my house early the following morning so that they could also listen to his story, for seeing and hearing is believing. Thus by the time Akara-Ogun returned, my house was packed full with no space to let any more in. I had already instructed my servants to prepare food for everyone, so before he began to recount his next story, I served all my guests with four basketfuls of corn meal and dishes of meat stew. After they had all eaten and drunk to repletion, Akara-Ogun started to relate his second story.

"My dear friends, I am pleased to see so many of you present today - young and old, male and female. It is a privilege to meet so many who hold my friend in such affection and high regard. When I came here yesterday only my friend was here. He welcomed me cordially and looked after me properly as a responsible host. It is my prayer, therefore, that the same sort of attitude will flourish among all the black races forever.

I have no doubt that my friend would have told you the history of my late parents and all about my experiences during my first visit to the Forest of Daemons of Irunmale. Now I'm sure that anyone who has listened to those accounts would have assumed that I should never dream of hunting there again – but if so, you were wrong. I did hunt there again, because I believe that one should practice what one has learned, and that one's actions should be guided by knowledge and experience. In any case, it would have been disagreeable for me at my age to suddenly throw up my occupation in favour of bricklaying or carpentry. But even granted that I remained a hunter, you will surely never have imagined that I would return to Irunmale Forest. Nevertheless, let me impress upon you, that is where I went and it should come as no surprise to any of you to learn that he who attempts what no one has attempted before should expect to experience what no one has experienced before. To justify this statement, I believe that no other hunter had visited the Forest of Daemons as frequently as I, and no other hunter could claim to have suffered as I had suffered. Moreover, to have experienced what I had, was no more than the natural consequence of my own actions for there is truth in the adage which says that 'Ambition destroys its possessor, for it obeys no law but its own appetite.' Therefore, I pray that none of you will become victims of your own making.

It was just a year after I had returned from my first expedition, that I picked up my gun and hunting bag one night, and went out hunting in Irunmale Forest again. The moon was very bright, and I thought it must be almost daybreak when I left home, not realizing it was still dead of night. By the time dawn was really breaking, I was only two hours walk from my destination. I hasten to add that this time I took a different route into the Forest of Daemons, hoping to avoid any recurrence of the unpleasantness which I had encountered on the first occasion.

I arrived at breakfast time and made a fire to roast a piece of yam. Once I had finished eating, I lit my tobacco pipe and relaxed. After I had enjoyed my smoke, I emptied out the tobacco, put the pipe back in my bag and surveyed my surroundings. For the first time I noticed two kola nut trees, though one had no nuts on it. As the other tree had kola nuts I plucked three pods. When I broke these open, I found ten nuts in all. I picked the biggest pod which happened to be multi-sectional, and after peeling and breaking it, I found there were four sections. This kind of nut is useful in the ritual of divination, especially when hunting, so I laid down my gun and cast the auspices, using the nut as a ritual offering. To my regret, the indications were unfavourable. For a successful hunt, when the kola nuts are cast up they should fall with two sections facing up and two facing down. I couldn't understand why they failed to fall that way today. However, after they had fallen badly on several occasions, I corrected them by turning them to the right configuration. "Man is the author of his own destiny," I told them, "hence, as this divination has failed to predict a good result, I shall take the necessary action to turn the divination into a favourable prediction, by and for myself." After I had done this, I picked up my gun and went to hunt for game in the forest.

As soon as I got up, I stumbled on my left foot, which is a psychic signal from my late mother, and a bad omen for me whenever it happens. It frightened me, and as I stood there pondering the significance of this unpleasant experience, a day-flying owl brushed my face with its wing – which as everyone knows, is a very bad omen indeed. I stood indecisively for about ten minutes, wondering about all these omens, but in the end I scorned death, exclaiming, "Ha ha! A man can only die once, so if I die it will be because my time has come." With that I resumed my journey into the forest to hunt. After a while I saw my first animal, which was a deer. Its back was towards me, and I waited in the hope that it would turn its head, but it didn't. In the end I shot it in the back, but the bullet failed to kill it; instead it left at a limping run. I pursued it vigorously over a long distance with my gun and cutlass, but was unable to catch up with it. Finally I saw it entering a cave and so I followed it inside.

The cave was big and very dark, and I couldn't see the deer, but I could hear its footsteps retreating in the distance. Then, after a certain point, I could no longer hear it either. This total disappearance surprised me, so I began to search for it everywhere. While I was thus preoccupied, someone suddenly seized my right arm, twisted it behind my back and began to shake me and slap my face very severely. As I struggled to free myself, he gripped me by the neck and squeezed it tightly while continuing to slap me with his other hand as he pushed me along.

After I had suffered considerably and could no longer bear it, I screamed, "Please let me go, and I promise I will never kill your deer again," and things of that kind; but he ignored my pleas, and continued to punish me as he pushed me along. Sometimes he pinched me, or worse still, knocked me on the head. The punishment took several forms, some worse than others, and during all this time I was unable to see him, as we were walking in total darkness.

After a while, we emerged from the cave and only then did I see the man. He was short, with a huge hunched back, and was covered in scales like a fish. He had two arms, two legs and two eyes like a human being, but he also had a short tail. His eyes were about six times the size as those of a human and the colour of fire. When we reached the open air, he told me to bend down and rest my hands on my knees. I did as he commanded. Then he mounted my back, gave me a kick, and demanded that I carry him about like a horse. Like it or not, I had no choice but to follow his instructions, as he had already seized my gun and hunting bag. It was made the more unpleasant because he began laughing and dribbling spittle all over my head and body.

We emerged into an open field where I suffered further severe punishment. He had a number of cut bamboo canes.

He thrashed me repeatedly whenever I tried to straighten my body. When I felt tired from the strain of carrying him, I had no choice but to plod along – except when he forced me to trot. If I made any sound which was not the sound of a horse, he slapped my face. He also commanded me to gallop like a horse which I had to obey, lest he thrash me even more with his cane.

After I had carried him about for some time, we came to a large cave where he dismounted and tied my hands together behind me with thick string. Then he brought a heavy chain from the cave and fastened it round my neck, though loose enough for me to breathe normally. He attached the other end to a big tree and went into the cave, which I supposed to be his home.

It must have been about two o'clock in the afternoon when I realized that he wasn't coming out again. I began to sob, but quietly, lest he came out and punish me for disturbing him. At about half past four he finally emerged from the cave and put his hand on my stomach to see if I was hungry. Deciding that I was, he brought me a chunk of raw yam. He cut it into small pieces which he laid before me on a broad leaf, and told me to bend down and pick them up with my mouth. I ate a few, but as I disliked the uncooked taste, I left the remainder. After I had eaten all that I was going to, he took the chain off my neck and the string from my hands and mounted me for another ride. It was about 7 o'clock by the time we got back, and once we were there, he ate some of the remaining pieces of raw

the cave, the hunched back fiend seized
Kara-Ogun and demanded to be carried on
his back, and to trot like a horse.

yam while I ate the rest. After that he tied my hands again and chained me to the tree as before and then went inside to sleep.

As you may imagine, I got no sleep throughout the night but spent the time thinking and sobbing bitterly at my own misfortune. In the morning he gave me more raw yam and rode me again until the evening which ended with a similar meal as before after which he tied me up and chained me to the tree again.

You might have thought that a man of my resource would have been able to free himself and escape, and ordinarily that would be true; but he had my gun and my hunting bag in the cave with him, and he never gave me any chance to go in there myself before he harnessed me by the neck to the big tree. I tried some of the spells in my possession, but none of them worked, nor did any of the incantations that I knew. After a while I finally realized the fundamental problem: I had disregarded the influence of God when I cast the nuts in a magical act against myself. I had forgotten that God has influence over everything that He has created, including herbs, roots and other elements. On the third day, therefore, I prayed to God:

"Almighty and ever-living God," I prayed, "I have no influence over the circumstances in which I find myself. Therefore, I need your help; please help me. I cannot handle this on my own; God, please help me. Please do not let me be the victim of this man's wishes. Do not let him kill me, and do not let me die in this forest, humiliated and without dignity. You are the only God that every worshipper calls upon in their supplications. The Muslims worship you as Allah and the Christians worship you as Jesus, all the days of their lives. Once again, I ask you to save me, for by nothing that I can devise can I save myself. Therefore I appeal to you, God, to save me."

That was what I said in my prayer that night, when I put my trust in God. In the morning, when the Scaly Man came to offer me the usual pieces of raw yam, I was inspired by God to ask him a question, as follows: "Please, master, I would be grateful to know why you do not cook the yam before you eat it."

He looked at me in astonishment, and admitted that he was quite unfamiliar with the idea of cooked yam, so I explained to him that cooked yam was far more delicious than uncooked. When he asked if I could cook a piece of yam for him, and I told him I could, he released me. I made a fire and cooked the yam for him, and when it was done I peeled the skin away and gave it to him to eat. When he had tasted it, he agreed that it was delicious, and started to talk to me more politely.

During our conversation the topic of my gun came up, and he asked me about its function. I explained that it was equipment for a pleasurable hobby, and that if I were to put my gun into anyone's mouth and gently caress it round the base, it would release copious, pure water into that person's mouth, so that he would not feel thirsty for seven days. At this he quickly brought my gun out of the cave. He eagerly thrust the muzzle into his mouth and asked me to start caressing it as described. I needed no encouragement, and as soon as I had it in position, I pulled the trigger. At the explosion, the Scaly Man fell dead.

That was how I killed the Scaly Man, but I didn't let that achievement go to my head, still being uncertain where I was. Even so, I went straight into his cave, where I found much valuable treasure, including coral and other semi-precious stones, fashionable coloured beads and bolts of different kinds of fabrics, including velvet, raw silk, cotton, batiks and traditional garments suitable for special occasions. I also found many different kinds of traditional hats, caps and other headgear, and three beautiful traditional crowns with veils of precious beads hanging down in front to protect the identity and privacy of the king wearing them.

Best of all, I found a good stock of yams, and cooked some for myself. Once I had finished eating, I selected some of the choicest treasures which I packed securely in my hunting bag. Then I picked up my gun and started looking for a familiar route which would lead me homewards. But unfortunately my problems were not over, for the more I sought the right direction, the more lost and benighted I became.

After I had become completely lost, I heard the sound of distant drumming in the forest and so headed in that direction. Once I got close, I discovered that it was coming from a village of elves, quite different from the elves that I had encountered previously. Both sexes looked like human beings, beautiful and elegantly clad. The Crown Prince of the elven Kingdom was holding a commemorative celebration, and I arrived to find everyone assembled in the market-place where their King's throne had been set up so that he could watch his son dancing on horseback.

By the time I got there, everyone was dancing round the prince. They were so immersed in what they were doing that no one noticed my presence except the King, who saw me in the distance and sent a messenger to summon me. I followed and when I saw the King, I prostrated myself on the ground and threw dust over my head in the customary gesture of respect. "Your Majesty," I said.

He commanded me to rise, and said, "Most of this world's elves hate human beings. They terrify them by day, and pursue them by night. They provoke them to anger, and then give them contempt. Nevertheless, it may interest you to know that I personally hate my fellow elves, and love humans because I admire their intelligence. Therefore, I want you to shed the load you are carrying on your head, and sit by my feet to watch the ceremony."

I was grateful for the King's welcome and sat down. Presently, I noticed that the drummers were off the beat, and asked if I might sit in with them. He granted my request and ordered the chief drummer to let me have a talking drum and to tell the rest of the band to be silent while I played it. I played with confidence as I had learnt how to drum as a boy when I had accompanied my brother who was a professional when not hunting with my father.

My virtuosity won me considerable respect among the elves. As long as I held the drum, they all danced to my music and, my dear friends; you can take my word, the elves are good dancers! I am also proud to add that I played the drum so well that the King got up from his throne and joined the dancing. I was very happy at their appreciation and kept drumming with great fervour as I moved closer to the King.

The dancing lasted a long time and when it was finally over, the King took me to his palace where a delicious meal was served. After we had finished eating, he offered me the gift of a house with a steward and a stewardess to look after me providing I would stay with him and make my home among the elves. He added that if I wanted to visit my family he would provide me with attendants to accompany me on the journey. But such visits could only be temporary and I would have to return. I could see the point of this stipulation, and accepted it.

I lived in the elf town for a long time and was very content. The King loved me dearly, and worked constantly to ensure that I felt happy, important and comfortable as if I was a member of his own family. Many of the townsfolk were equally kind and friendly towards me, while I myself did the best I could to please everyone. I would never refuse a request for help, nor would I ever refuse to go wherever the King chose to send me. It was as if we were children of the same mother.

There's a saying that however many wives a man may have, one will always be his favourite. So it is the same with friendship. I had one friend who was closer than any other; a well known and highly influential citizen. One day this friend visited me and said, "Akara-Ogun, did you know that the people were planning to assassinate the King?" I did not, so he gave me the details. They had all entered into a conspiracy with his favourite wife to whom they had given a kola nut. She was to give the nut to the King, and the King would certainly die if he tasted it. The people had been planning this murder for a long time, but it had only been finalized the previous day, which was why he was bringing it to my attention now.

I was horrified by the news, and went straight to the King to warn him of it. He disbelieved me at first, because he trusted the woman, but in the end he agreed that if she should offer him a kola nut, he would keep it safe instead of eating it.

Next morning, after the King and his wife had finished breakfast, she said, "Your Majesty, I forgot to mention to you that yesterday, that another of your queens and I visited a friend of yours who gave us four kola nuts. Two of them were my share, and since you know that I could never eat anything without sharing it with you, I have eaten mine but have been keeping yours wrapped in a leaf. I wanted to give it to you yesterday, but forgot, but now I'm glad, for the perfect time to eat a kola nut is after finishing a meal like this. Here is the nut, my darling, and I hope you will eat it with pleasure." As soon as she had finished speaking she offered the nut to the King, but instead of eating it he kept it hidden, and pretended he had eaten it.

It was a surprise to all that the King suffered no stomach upset, nor any other kind of ill health throughout that day or the next. Indeed, he was still going strong a week later, so the people called a meeting and summoned the queen to enquire what had gone wrong. She described how she had given the kola nut to the King, and proposed a new plan, and her reasons for taking part:

'I don't want you to think I would ever deceive you, and I also want to impress it on you that I have never benefited at all from this man since he first proposed marriage to me. Those who see me in public may think that he is meeting my needs, but that is not the case. He may be rich, but he is ever so stingy when it comes to parting with money! One is thankful for the shoulders that anchor a dress and prevent it from falling from the body; so by the same token I am grateful to my mother who has been my help in times of need. I would have suffered terribly from deprivation and humiliation in this place had it not been for my mother who took care of me. For this man is not only desperately stingy, he is also an aesthete. He loves beautiful things, and whenever he visits a foreign country he makes a point of noticing how the queens of those countries dress and conduct themselves. Then he rushes home and attempts to improve my image by buying me new clothes like theirs. He is an irresponsible and awkward man, who deserves to be assassinated.

This is how the plan should go, and it's quite simple. Tonight, when everybody is asleep, I will open the gates of the palace. There should be four strong men with cutlasses waiting outside. They should enter the King's room, in which windows will be left open and then kill whoever they find there.'

That is what the woman said, as she conspired to betray her husband because of disagreements over money. I pray that the Merciful God will not allow any man in this audience to fall foul of such a wicked woman.

My house was in the palace compound and it took some time for me to hear about this second conspiracy, but as soon as I did I went straight to the King's residence. When I got to the back yard behind the room where the King and this wicked woman normally slept, I sat on the ground and kept watch to see if one of the windows would soon be opened. Just as I expected, I soon saw her opening a window, and it nearly hit my head as it swung out. Then she opened the doors into the room, and the doors leading out of the palace. I watched her doing this, and as soon as she went out towards the main gate I went to wake the King and took him by the hand. When he recognized me he wanted to talk, but I signalled to him to keep quiet and led him out to my own house, where I asked him to sleep, which he did. Then I went back to his room and shut the window. Soon after that, the woman returned to sleep in another room.

When I knew she was deeply asleep and had been snoring for some time, I quietly opened a window and left. I didn't go home, but hid behind the angle of another house in the compound, from where I could see what was going on.

I had barely settled when I saw the four strong men enter, cutlasses in their hands, and head towards the King's residence. I got up and followed them stealthily. Once they saw the open window they rushed into the room and in an instant, most regrettably killed the woman. They cut her entire body into small pieces, hoping to have killed the King, but they were misguided in that assumption, for as a man sows, so also does he reap! The evil that men do, most definitely live after them, for thus did that wicked woman die, painfully and sordidly, even as the Almighty God saved that good King from becoming the victim of her conspiracy.

The King himself was quite baffled by my actions, but I explained everything to him the following morning. When he heard what had happened he was quite terrified, but nonetheless praised God and thanked me. After that, I suggested that he go and retrieve the kola nut that the woman had given him the other day. When he went to investigate, he found that the kola nut had become a bunch of palm-nuts - a remarkable transformation! Had he eaten that nut, it would have germinated inside him like a yam tuber!

Thus did the King survive the second attempt on his life, but there was a third yet to come.

There was a notorious one-eyed tiger in this Kingdom which terrorized the people, eating one now and again as it pleased, and had proved impossible to kill despite all efforts. The people of the Kingdom unanimously decided to summon all the medicine men together for a meeting and formed a conspiracy with them. The idea was to ask the King to summon everyone in the Kingdom to assemble in the market square of the capital on a specified day, so as to receive an important message from the genies. Once this was done, assuming that the King agreed to issue the summons and the entire population responded, the chief medicine man would then rise and address the people. His speech was to go as follows:

"Greetings, ladies and gentlemen. We have called this meeting to discuss the problem of the one-eyed tiger with you. The genies have now told us that if we don't want the beast to plague us any more, we should summon everybody to a meeting where we must select someone as a blood-offering to the tiger. The person selected will serve as atonement for the sins of all the people of the Kingdom. Moreover, the person so selected will have to volunteer himself as no force may be used to select anyone. The genies also said that if from among ourselves we failed to find a volunteer prepared to sacrifice his life for the good of the Kingdom, then we would be forced to offer our own King whether we like it or not. If we failed to carry out this last instruction, instead of this one beast we would be plagued by seven beasts, each of which would have a hundred horns. It therefore behoves us to consider this matter carefully."

It is obvious that these people had formed a diabolical plot without realizing that their efforts must be in vain, for the power of God lay in the person whom they were conspiring against. Consider what the chief medicine man had been asked to say! They knew very well that it would be difficult for the King to get out of this situation because no one had ever seen the genies, and no one would be prepared to die for no good reason. Nevertheless, the entire population of the Kingdom was present when this decision was made, except for myself, the King, one of the queens, two princes and the King's personal servant.

Thus, when the medicine men came to discuss their plan with the King he did as they recommended without realizing their true intention. He summoned everyone to the meeting, and when they were all settled, the chief medicine man got up to speak as he had been instructed. As soon as he had finished his speech he asked the audience if there was anyone prepared to volunteer to die; no one responded, but all remained seated and looked round at each other. After this had gone on for a few minutes the King got up to announce that since no one else had volunteered, he was prepared to offer himself to be killed by the beast. The people were delighted by the news and hypocritically thanked the king!

I waited patiently for the King to finish his speech, and as soon as he sat down I got up to speak as follows: "Your Majesty, you are not going to die such a death. I will volunteer in your stead, and I am prepared to die."

When I had finished speaking, the King turned to me and wept. He appealed to me not to go, but my mind was made up. He repeated this appeal several times, but I took no notice and said I would definitely go. I got up immediately, and asked the elves to take me to be killed by the beast. They were all very angry and showed me no sympathy, saying that I was responsible for my own misfortune. But just before I set out, I sent for my cutlass and my sharp stabbing-knife. They were brought to me at once, but the elves laughed at me with great scorn because they reckoned that hunters far more experienced than myself had been unable to kill such a dangerous beast.

Soon we reached the cave, which was in a large hollow under a great rock. There I drew my cutlass and my sharp knife, pulled up my trousers in readiness and conjured that the claws of the beast should recede. Finally I entered the cave in search of the beast. Fortunately I had cast my spell successfully, and its claws had receded by the time I found it. When it saw me, it turned towards me and attacked. I was terrified by the sight of the one-eyed beast, yet I was equally determined to try my best to overpower it before it could kill me, so I kept a tight grip on my knife.

Just before it reached me it pounced as a hawk would dive on a chicken, but I made no attempt to retreat. Even before it pounced I had determined to damage its eyesight by aiming the point of my knife at its eye. As it leapt, I caught its eye with my knife and stabbed deep into it. Then I backed a few steps away from the angry beast. I was unable to withdraw my knife, but fortunately I had succeeded in blinding it. The piercing pain penetrated deep into its body, enraging it further as it searched for me. Had it caught me, then the outcome would have been tragic for me. Nevertheless, once I realized it was getting tired I moved closer, hoping to seize it by the neck and twist it backwards so that I could pin its back to the ground and stab it with my knife. But it threw me off in its fury and I landed prone on a rock.

It rushed forwards to catch me where I had fallen, but missed, giving me time to get up. I could see it was tiring, so once I was on my feet, I crept up on it with my cutlass and stabbed it in the neck with all my strength, which did some damage. Then I caught hold of it and we wrestled for some time, knocking each other down on several occasions. In the end the beast fled, but I held onto it with both hands as it dragged me about the cave. This lasted for about five minutes before it stopped, panting heavily. I could see how tired it was, so I seized it by the wound in its neck and pulled with all my strength. It lost balance and fell on its back, and before it could struggle to its feet, I reached for my cutlass and stabbed it in the belly, deep enough for its intestines to fall out. Thus did I kill that wicked beast.

Once I had killed the one-eyed tiger, I had the problem of dragging it out of the cave, for if I failed in that the elves would not be able to see it, and my achievement would not be appreciated. I took it by the legs and pulled with all my strength, but it hardly moved, being very heavy. At first I was afraid I would never be able to get the beast out, but I felt I must give it my best effort before I gave up the struggle. First I sat down to rest a while. Then I strapped my knife and cutlass back on to my belt and once again pulled the beast by the legs with all my strength. This time I managed to move it, and dragged it into town at about six o'clock in the evening, to the great excitement and amazement of everyone who saw me!

The King had assumed I was dead, and had been in tears ever since I went into the cave, So had those who had accompanied me to the cave and then waited outside. After I had failed to come out after a reasonable interval, they had returned home and told everyone I had been killed.

The King's joy at seeing me alive was quite indescribable, and thereafter I became his closest friend and advisor, whom he consulted on all matters. Whatever I decreed became law in that town. But the more I advanced myself, the more people took offence at my cordial relationship with the King, and I could see no solution to this problem. People were constantly trying to sow discord between us, by telling him all sorts of nonsensical stories about me, and plotting against me, but he never took any notice.

The King owned a very unusual dog with teeth of gold and hair made .of brass which had been presented to him as a coronation gift by Sokoti, the Smith of Heaven. The King was greatly attached to this dog, and had vowed that if ever he caught anyone ill-treating it, he would give that person over to the mercy of the young men of the town, who could treat him as severely as they liked.

I had looked after the dog ever since I had come to live there, and had never let it suffer any ill treatment, so it was quite used to me. But unfortunately it disappeared one day.

I went to the King to ask if he knew where it was, but he said he had no idea. He and I both searched for it most diligently, but we couldn't find it. In the end the King had the town crier summon everybody to a meeting in the market place. There he had set up his throne, and I stood at his right hand. Once everyone was settled, he told them how deeply he regretted the loss of the dog which had been presented to him by Sokoti, the Smith of Heaven, on his coronation day, and how neither he nor I had been able to find it. He appealed to all the people to help him find the dog.

He had hardly finished speaking when a man got up to speak in reply. "Your Majesty the King," he began, "may God grant you long life and may he give you good health! I pray also that God may protect you from falling victim to your enemies, both known and unknown, and that you continue to prosper and progress in all things, without hindrance from any quarter. I thank you for bringing this matter to the attention of the people, for it is certain that anyone who knew how greatly you treasure that dog will feel sympathy for you. But there is one thing which I would like everyone to be aware of. The dog has most definitely been stolen, and the thief must be a close friend of the King. I think that if this matter is properly investigated, we should find out who first informed the King that the dog was missing. That same person should be held responsible for its recovery, since as he was the first to know that the dog was missing, he should therefore know where the dog was lost. Long live the King!"

As soon as he had finished speaking, another man got up to speak in his support, saying that he was right, and that they should question the person who first informed the King that the dog was missing. Everyone knew they were referring to me.

The third person to speak was my closest friend, the same who had in the past, been informing me of their plans. He began his address thus: "Hello, ladies and gentlemen, greetings to you all, and I pray we don't have to keep on gathering here for similar reasons. Ah! Ah! As a familiar proverb says; a witch cries today and a child dies tomorrow – meaning that nothing ever happens by coincidence and no matter what has happened, preceding events will always have furnished omens. No one should therefore be in any doubt that Akara-Ogun is the person that stole the dog. I should know this, for I am his closest friend. He had been planning the theft for some time before he finally stole the dog last night. At the time I warned him of the possible consequences, but he paid me no heed – for he's a thief by profession. I suggest that the people of this town deal with him accordingly. He's completely irresponsible, and I shall never be his friend again since I don't want him to get me into trouble."

After this he then turned to me and said, "Aha! Behold the thief! When I warned you not to steal, did you pay any heed? When I warned you not to make any comment, did you stop talking? When I warned you not to be greedy, did you moderate your behaviour? When you first arrived here you were a nobody, but soon you were more confident. Now you swan around like a member of the nobility, and associate with a foreign King. Don't you know that shame treads on the heels of the greedy, and that every beginning has an end? You are a stupid man, and today your time has run out. The King must definitely fulfil his promise and hand you over to the youths for summary justice."

My dear friends, I must tell you I was frightened when I heard what this man said, and as I opened my mouth to reply, a torrent of tears began to flow down my cheeks, for he had been my closest friend in the town. We had been so close that whatever he said about me would surely be believed by all, even though what he was saying now was not true. Nevertheless, I summoned up my courage and began to speak.

"It is certainly true that there are no honest persons anymore, and only a few people can be trusted in this world. I had to befriend several people in case I found myself in an unfriendly place, so that if half of them let me down, I could, at least, depend on the loving support of the other half. Alas! I thought you were my best and most reliable friend, but now I can see that you are one of those who plot against me. I don't blame you for that – I blame myself for my unsound judgement, particularly in choosing such an unreliable person as you for a friend. I may have set in train consequences which I failed to foresee, but there can be no doubt that anyone who fails to take precautions shall suffer the consequences that follow. A man must reap as he has sown, and before I die today, I will teach you a lesson."

As I was saying this, I was reaching for my pointed knife which I kept strapped to my waist, and as soon as I had finished speaking I drew it and stabbed him to death. I could see that the elders were angry at this, so I leapt into their midst and stabbed them all to death except for the King. After that, I ordered the youths to bury the corpses, but when they tried to do so, the ground turned to solid rock making digging impossible. This was a sign that Earth had rejected them as sinners. Having seen this, I ordered the youths to throw the corpses into the sea, but the sea also rejected them, and washed them ashore. Then I told the youths to hang them from trees, but the trees also rejected them, and as soon as a corpse was hung on a tree, it fell off. Then a chain dropped from Heaven and tied them all together, leaving them suspended in the air! There they stayed, rotting, and desecrated by carrion birds.

I did not realize at the time that the youths resented what I had forced them to do as they made no attempt to challenge my authority. When it became dark they went home and I did the same.

I woke up late the following morning with the sun already up. As I rose from my sleeping mat to go outside, I saw a great crowd of citizens coming towards me armed with clubs and cutlasses. It never occurred to me that they might be coming after me, and before I understood what was happening they were upon me. I had only a coverlet wrapped round my body, but before I had the chance to go inside and get dressed, they took hold of me. They twisted my hands behind my back and tied them tightly; then they went into my house to take away all my treasures, including both the valuables which I had acquired since I had been living there and those which I had brought with me. They tied them up in bundles to be carried away on the heads of the children while they led me to the market place thrashing me with canes as they went so that my body was badly bruised by the time we got there.

They told me to get into a pit which had been specially dug for what they intended to do to me, and I had no choice but to obey. It was deep enough to cover my body up to my neck, with only my head showing clear above the ground. I was made to stand straight and they filled the pit with sand, which they pounded hard to compress it round my body. They carried on with this until the pit was completely filled, with only my head showing clear. Then they shaved off all my hair with a knife, and once my scalp showed fairly clean and smooth, they poured honey over it. Soon a swarm of flies was buzzing round, feeding on it. Having done this they laid all my possessions out in front of me, together with some food, and a notice for me to read:

You can look, but you can't taste!

Thus was I subjected to varying forms of punishment. I wept and pleaded for mercy time and time again, but my pleas fell on deaf ears. They showed me no compassion, but just kept on yelling. In the end they got bored and

Buried with my head above ground,
they poured honey on my head that
caused flies to buzz around me.

left me alone. By this time I had lost all hope of surviving and resigned myself to death, but God had seen their wickedness and decided to set me free. I had been buried at about half-past eleven in the morning, but it became cloudy at about two in the afternoon, and shortly after that it began to rain. It was very heavy, and didn't stop until eight in the evening. I was out in the rain for the entire period, but though this heavy rain was a great torment to me, it proved a blessing in disguise, for when it stopped I realized that the soil had been softened. I wriggled my body to see if I could get out. I soon found out that it might be possible and so after I had struggled for a considerable time I finally climbed out of the pit. I immediately packed some of my most valuable possessions and ate some of the food which had been placed in front of me. Then I picked up my pack and made a hurried departure from that town under cover of darkness.

My injuries prevented me from walking very far, but after a short distance I came upon a large subterranean trench and went inside. I recognized it as the trench where the townsfolk dumped their dead animals as it was their custom not to eat animals which had died from unknown causes. I stepped on a decomposing carcass as soon as I entered the trench, which was full of them and their stench. After I had wandered around for a while, I came upon the carcass of a goat which I thought had only just been dumped there. Its bloated body gave a deceptively firm appearance, and I needed to sit down. But it must have been dead for at least four days. As I settled down, it burst open and the liquid from inside sprayed over my buttocks!

With this and all the other unpleasant experiences I had been through, I burst into tears, and I have to say, I wished I was dead. Fortunately for me, God had compassion on me, and sent me help in the form of a beautiful woman. She came up to me, took me by the hand to comfort me, and after pulling me up, she asked me to follow her. I went with her while still weeping, and after we had gone a short way through the subterranean trench, we came to a lovely house. It was full of boys and girls, who were all very beautiful. It turned out that the woman was the matron of the household. As soon as we got inside, she ordered her attendants to bathe me in warm water and oil my skin with perfumed ointment. After that she gave me a beautiful velvet coverlet to wrap round my body and delicious food to eat. After I had finished eating, I prostrated myself before her in gratitude for what she had done, but she told me there was no need for that. Then she took me into another room where there was a bed and asked me to lie down. This I did, and immediately fell asleep. I didn't wake up until the following afternoon, when she came to rouse me and give me breakfast.

The woman looked after me so wonderfully that by the second day I could even say that Irunmale Forest was the best place to hunt. I must also add that when comfort comes, bad memories vanish. Such a sentimental reaction was natural in my present state of mind, and my current pleasure caused my recent unpleasant experiences to fade. Even so, what the woman did for me on the third day was beyond description.

On the evening of the third day she complained of a headache. I sat closer to her, let her rest her head on my arm and began to recite some incantations which I believed would make her feel better. But, my dear comrades, I regret to say that the woman died in my arms while I was still reciting the incantations. As soon as she died a bell rang, and all the people of her household came hurrying in to die in my presence. At this point I wanted to die too, but was unable to do so. What kind of experience might this be I asked myself.

I was unable to sleep throughout that night, being the only living creature among all those dead, and to be honest, I was frightened of the dead. I therefore called upon the spirit of my dead mother very early in the morning, and asked her to come down from Heaven and rescue me from my present circumstances. There was no response, so I repeated my call. On the third attempt, therefore, I raised my voice in anguish and cried, "Ah! My mother, my mother, my mother! Why don't you respond to my call? Why can I not feel your presence? Would it not be more honourable to die than to suffer humiliation of this kind? It would have been better for me to have died at home than to suffer like this. Do I have to die in this wilderness? Is it good that I should have no known grave? I am your only surviving son, but I cannot say that my life brings me any benefit, because I keep suffering humiliation and other unpleasant experiences in a life which offers neither stability nor hope. Ah, my dear mother, my very own mother, an able mother, a responsible mother, a mother indeed! A good mother, a gentle mother on Earth, a famous mother in Heaven and a prosperous mother! Ah! You perfect mother, wherever you may be today, please let me feel your presence!"

As soon as I had finished this imprecation, the ground cracked open and my late mother appeared before me. She found me weeping, and she too started to cry. She hugged me and patted me on the head, and said, "Why are you calling me, my son? Tell me, please tell me. I do want you to tell me, my son. I knew that you were fated to encounter some difficulties in life, because you were destined to be a brave and famous man in this world. It is my prayer that God will not deprive you of long life, and that your Creator will not deprive you of the opportunity to become rich. But try to live an exemplary life before you die, and leave this world a better place than you found it. With regard to your journey, you will definitely return home, and you will not die prematurely. Moreover, you will enjoy a pleasant and respectable life into old age, because there is nothing worse than to see an old person suffering unnecessarily. Therefore, tell me if there is an important matter that has caused you to request my presence at this moment, and I will do my best to help you."

When my mother had finished speaking I wiped off my tears and told her I had called for her help because I feared that I would not be able to get out of this place. I told her of the various misfortunes which I had recently encountered, after which she offered me a delicious cake which I ate. When I had finished eating, she asked me to follow her which I did. We had not gone very far when we reached a big cave. Here, she took a smooth, snow-white pebble from her pocket and give it to me. She told me that as soon as she had gone I must throw the pebble into the cave, and follow it wherever it rolled. She assured me that if I followed her instructions I would soon come out at the other end of the Forest of Daemons where I would meet another hunter who had been lost there a long time ago. She also promised that I would not have many problems between leaving the forest and arriving home. As soon as she had finished speaking, the Earth opened and swallowed her up again, and I began to follow the instructions she had given me.

CHAPTER 4

Akara-Ogun and Lamorin

I emerged from the cave after about an hour. While there, I picked up the white pebble which I put in my hunting bag. Throughout all the difficulties I had experienced, I had never parted from my gun and bag. As soon as I came out, I met a man whose name was Lamorin who told me that he had been lost in this notorious hunting forest for the past three years. He was very happy to see me because he was my neighbour in my home town, and after affectionate greetings, we shared our experiences. My own were of little weight compared with his, since he had been lost in the forest and without contact with home for such a long time.

We set off together on foot, presently coming to a river. As we walked along the bank, we saw a big man ahead of us. He was stark naked except for a large bag which he carried over his shoulder, and was eating a lion's head. As soon as he saw us, he dropped the lion's head and came towards us. Lamorin urged me loudly to run away and when I demanded to know why, he replied that the man confronting us was Ijamba [Peril], the father of Adanu [Loss] who lived with him in Starvation House. Having learned this, I needed no further persuasion and we ran for our lives with Ijamba in hot pursuit. Soon I became separated from them both, so I climbed a tree with my gun and bag, hoping to spot one or the other.

Shortly after I had taken up my position on the tree, I spotted Ijamba heading towards me, looking intently for us wherever we might be. When he came close to my hiding place, he began to exclaim, "O dear me! O dear me! How unfortunate that those two well nourished creatures have vanished like that! What am I going to eat for my supper tonight? O dear me!" Shortly after he had finished these words, he looked up and saw me. Ah ha! He was happy at that! He stretched out his long arm to pluck me from the tree, and put me in his shoulder-bag. I kept calm, confident because I had my gun with me. I carefully loaded it with the heaviest bullets I had and put it to one side, ready for immediate use while I tried to relax. When I was sufficiently rested, I shot him in the skull and he fell dead. That was how I killed Ijamba. Once he was dead, I called out to Lamorin who was very happy to see Ijamba lying on the ground like a log.

We went back to the camp Lamorin had built where we would sleep that night. After we had finished cooking our meal and were about to eat, a tall man arrived to join us. He greeted us and sat down to eat with us, but as soon as I saw him, I recognized him as an elf. After he had taken two morsels there was very little left on the plate which annoyed me, so I carefully lifted a very hot slab of potsherd from the fire and hit him in the neck with it. He walked away screaming. The next day we saw the potsherd wrapped round a teak tree. How a potsherd that was stuck in the neck of an elf found its way there, remains a mystery to me. Nevertheless, despite the encounter with the elf, we both slept in the camp again that night. The following morning after we had greeted each other and eaten our breakfast, Lamorin and I took our guns and went out to hunt separately.

I had not gone far when I saw a one-legged man sleeping under a tree, with his walking-stick leaning against it. I crept closer to get hold of the walking-stick, intending to take it away so as to find out how well he could walk without it, when he woke up. Unfortunately when my hand touched the walking-stick, it triggered a warning signal which woke the man up immediately, but before he could respond I had already run away with it and was triumphantly yelling at him from a safe distance in celebration of having captured it successfully. He pleaded with me for some time, but I refused to return it until he had promised to give me a magic hunting spell. Then he spoke to me as follows.

"My name is Aroni [Cripple], the one-legged elf. My house is well stocked with good and evil things. I was once the wickedest of all the elves that had rebelled against God. King Solomon the Great warned me but I paid him no heed. I showed no regard for God either which is why He turned me into a one-legged creature in punishment. I have lived on Earth for about a thousand years, but my nature remains the same, for which reason God said to me in His wrath, 'I will leave you alone until the time when you will be dealt with by Death, who lives in Heaven above.' I am now awaiting my fate from Death. Therefore, I appeal to you to give me back my walking-stick and I will do you a favour in return."

I felt sorry for him after hearing this and gave the stick back. In return, he gave me a magic spell in the form of a powder, and told me to sprinkle it on an animal's footprints. Whichever animal had made the print, that animal would return to die on the spot. When I tested the spell I found it worked just as predicted, but I didn't make use of it all the time, since I was afraid of using it up too quickly.

I had only walked a short distance from this elf when I met a strange creature no more than two feet high and with two heads. He also had two horns, one on each side of the heads, but only one eye located on his chest. I greeted him, and he responded courteously. His voice was very clear and stereophonic because he spoke with two mouths at the same time.

"Where are you from, and where are you going to?" I enquired.

He replied, saying, "Why do you want to know about me?"

I answered, "I notice how short you are, and I also observe that you carry two heads."

He responded to my observation, saying, "It is true that I have two heads, and that I am very short. My name is Kurembete [Dwarf] and I live on the far side of Heaven.

I was once one of the angels most beloved by God, but I rebelled against God's law and His doctrine and caused much trouble in Heaven. God realized that I was troublesome and full of evil thoughts, so He handed me over to Satan to be punished by being cast into Hell fire for exactly seven years. When I went back to God after the seventh year, he noticed no significant sign of repentance in me, and said in His wrath: 'You are a nuisance, you thin little creature; you rebelled against Me, yet you are of no significance. I shall therefore divide your head into two halves from this day forth, and you shall speak in different tongues with speech as complex and diverse as I imposed on the people who built the Tower of Babel, when they showed no regard for Me. I shall cast you into a wild forest, where you will wander about aimlessly and without rest throughout your life until someone brings your life to an end by throwing soil at you.' So it has been with me ever since, kind hunter. I appeal to you, therefore, to scoop up a handful of soil from the ground and throw it at me, for I am tired of wandering about." I felt sorry for him, so I scooped up a handful of soil and threw it at him. He immediately turned into a big rock, which has remained permanently in the same spot ever since.

After this incident I lost my fear and respect for the elves and went about my business regardless. As I was wandering about in the forest, I suddenly met a beautiful woman and have to admit that I immediately became infatuated with her. I greeted her, and she responded, but when I asked her how she came to be in such a forest as this, she gave no reply to such a personal question. In the end I pleaded with her to become my wife, but she declined. I pleaded again and yet again, but she still refused. Finally I threatened to shoot her if she still refused to marry me, but she replied that my gunshot could do her no harm whatsoever. Enraged, I pointed my gun at her and pulled the trigger; there was a distinct report, but no bullet emerged. She looked at me long and hard, and remarked, "If it were not for the compassion that I have for you today, I would have killed you at once." I immediately replied that she could do me no harm, and with no further words on either side she turned her back on me and went on her way.

I was so bewitched by her beauty that I could not help following her and taking her by the hand. As she turned to look at me she fell down and turned into a large tree, but I still held onto the tree because I had liked the woman so much. At this, the tree transformed itself into a deer with long horns on its head, but I still kept hold of her, though she struggled hard. As she was unable to break my grip, she turned into a burning fire, but I still didn't let go, and the fire didn't burn me. She continued to transform herself into all sorts of things, including a big bird, a pool of water and a huge snake, but I held on tight, and eventually she turned back into a beautiful woman as before. She looked at me, smiled and said, "I will marry you, brave hunter." Indeed she did marry me, and Lamorin was the officiating priest who solemnized the marriage. I celebrated the wedding by throwing a great feast, and it was a very grand occasion because when a man is married to an elf, every creature must be well fed.

Lamorin and I were great friends and so fond of each other's company that we hated to be parted for a moment. But one day while hunting in the forest, we were still on the trail when night was falling. Unfortunately we had run out of oil for our lamps, so were lucky that the moonlight was as bright as day. After we had been walking in the moonlight for a while, we came to a cliff with many caves. The paths leading into the caves were very smooth and Lamorin said he was going to sleep in one of them. I warned him not to do so, but he was determined. After he had gone inside, I quickly climbed a large tree to relax and watch what was going on around me. Soon I noticed a big man who had four eyes, six hands and two horns an his head coming out of the cave carrying a broken calabash full of blood to a tree which grew in front of the cliff. He addressed it as follows.

"I thank you today, my Lord, for I know it was you who directed this animal to me in this place, and I pray that this opportunity may come to me regularly. Once again, I thank you."

That was all I saw. I waited until the morning, but Lamorin didn't come out. I called to him, but there was no reply, so I got down from the tree where I had spent the night and went back to the camp to tell my wife. Since she was not human, she knew immediately what must have happened to Lamorin.

"Alas!" she cried, "The man you saw is called Tembelekun [Rebellion], and his elder brother's name is Bilisi [Evil] who lives in the Bottomless Pit where my own mother was born. Tembelekun is married to my younger sister and they have a son called Idarudapo [Chaos]. When that son grew to manhood he took service with Satan, the King of Hell. I have learnt that Idarudapo has been very diligent in his duties, in recognition of which he has won promotion to high office. I am also happy to learn that he is at present the Chief of those who refuel Hellfire.

"What I most dislike about his colleagues at Hellfire is that their employment pollutes their bodies and minds, making them as black as charcoal and very cruel. Therefore, my husband, I greatly fear that Lamorin has fallen victim to Tembelekun, because he feeds exclusively on human flesh. What a pity!"

When she had finished this I began to weep bitterly, with torrents of tears cascading from my eyes. I roared like a lion, my cries shook the forest, but no amount of lamentation could bring back my friend.

I had been with Lamorin since my late mother had rescued me after my second adventure astray in this wilderness, and I had enjoyed myself so much in the Forest of Daemons that I had never bothered to go home. But now, with his unfortunate death, I lost my taste for the place, and tried to find my way home.

One day, hunting in the forest, I discovered a narrow pathway. It attracted me, so I set off to investigate where it might lead. I walked a long way, though it seemed that it was never going to end, but I was determined to pursue it to its end. At noon exactly, I arrived at a hut and went inside where I found a child. When I took a close look at the child, I recognized him as my first cousin, the child of my maternal uncle. I was very happy at this unexpected encounter, but nevertheless I called out for my uncle, who was then at a nearby farm. When he heard, he came and embraced me very happily. He then asked me where I had been and why I had stayed away so long, but before replying, I asked him to excuse me so that I could go and collect my belongings and my wife, to which he agreed. I then went back to the camp for my wife.

I had been walking for about ten minutes when I met her on the trail. I was surprised to see her, as I had left her behind at the camp, but I greeted her, saying, "My dear wife, I am surprised to see you here. I hope there is nothing wrong."

She answered, "My darling, my darling, my dearest darling, I would never have believed that our relationship could end like this. I had been keeping an eye on you until you got to the hut where you found members of your family. Being an elf, I cannot share my life with human beings because they are always preoccupied with evil thoughts. Please take this scrap of cloth as a gift from me. Whenever you feel hungry, ask this cloth for whatever you desire to eat, and it shall give it to you. I would never have imagined that the strong bond of love between us would suddenly end like this. Ah! My dearest sweetheart, please don't forget me until you die – now I must go."

As soon as she had finished, a man suddenly appeared and took her by the hand. "My dear sister," he said, "please hurry up; let us return to our home in the Bottomless Pit." With that they both vanished, but I found the scrap on the ground and picked it up. Whenever I felt hungry I asked the cloth, and my house was filled with plenty of food.

I was sad that my wife had vanished like that, but I went back to the camp to collect the valuables I had acquired since I had been lost in the forest, and returned to my uncle's hut, from where I finally returned home. Thus ends the story of my second visit to that terrible forest.

Once I was home I laid down my gun and promised myself never to go hunting again, nor to undertake any other difficult task, for two reasons: first, because of the various problems which I had encountered there, and secondly because the articles which I had brought back with me from this second foray were so many and valuable that when I sold them I became the richest person in the whole town, more wealthy than even the King. I am afraid, that is the end of this story as I have said before and since it is almost night time, I must now go home, hoping to come back tomorrow to tell you the rest of what happened.

When Akara-Ogun had finished his story he ate some food and then shook hands with all those who had come to listen to his story. I then walked with him a short distance to see him off before we shook hands and bade each other farewell, saying, "Good night and God bless till we meet again tomorrow."

CHAPTER 5

The Delegates to Mount Langbodo

The news that an elderly man had been coming to my house to tell me unusual stories had spread all round the town, so the following morning the whole town was there. They came in droves, and took up all the space in my house! I laid out several mats on the ground outside for people to sit on but soon ran out of those so I started to borrow mats wherever I could. I got about a hundred and fifty before I gave up, but even these were not sufficient, so much of the audience had to stand. Others climbed trees or sat on the roof. The effect was like a great flock of palm-birds perching on palm-trees.

Soon Akara-Ogun arrived, and when he saw us he said: "I have something new to tell you today, which will be completely different from what I told you yesterday. Therefore I want every one of you to get ready to listen."

We all fell silent waiting to hear what he had to say. He continued his story thus: "Ah! The works of God are innumerable, like the grains of sand on a beach! I must say that I felt threatened when I first saw you all, but my fear disappeared when I moved closer and felt more comfortable with you. The first thought that came to my mind on that occasion was that by the time every one of you has died, there would not be sufficient teak trees in the forest to make coffins for such a multitude! But on later reflection, I felt more optimistic that not all of you would die by natural causes."

This last statement was offensive to the audience who all began to clamour, "I will *surely* die a natural death! *I* will surely die a natural death!" But he appealed to them to hold on and listen to his explanation, as follows.

"Truth is bitter, and the world hates those who are honest. Nevertheless, I would like to ask you four questions, and if you can answer them, it will mean that I was wrong in the statement I just made. On the other hand, if you fail to answer correctly, it will mean that you misunderstood me. These are my questions.

"I would like someone from the audience to tell me exactly when he will die. After that I would like the same person to tell me how he will die – whether it will be through illness, killed by a falling tree, drowned in the river or whatever. Moreover, I would like to know where that person is going to die – whether at home or in the forest, on the road or in the bedroom, abroad or in this country? The fourth question is this: that person must tell me in full detail all that will happen to him from this moment until he dies. He should remember to say when he shall stumble, fall sick, suffer bereavement, quarrel with others, and state how many enemies he has had in the past, and how many more he will have for the rest of his lifetime. He should also bear in mind that not everybody we see can be said to be in good health, and that it is easy to recognise what oneself desires, but difficult, if not impossible, to know what someone else desires."

When he had finished speaking no one could give any answer to his questions, because no one knew when, how, where or what would happen to him before his death. Seeing that we were all quiet, he said, "Ah ha! I notice that you are all quiet, and the reason why you keep quiet is this – the mystery of life can only be unlocked by God, and if people could unravel the mystery, there would never have been any illness, poverty, trouble or even servants, because everybody would be master in his own house – and the state of the world would be very much worse than it is now!"

We were greatly amazed by this speech, which touched on very deep topics. Accordingly, we changed our views, and began to say things like, "What you have said is true," and "We would like you to carry on, sir," and "You are quite right, sir, please carry on." With these assurances, the man continued his story.

My dear comrades, I have gone through Hell and high seas, I have amassed a great deal of experience of life, and there is nothing in this world that I am afraid of. I told you yesterday about my unpleasant adventures during my second visit to Irunmale Forest, rightly called the Forest of Daemons, and I also mentioned how I swore never to hunt again, nor to undertake any difficult task. But I would like to tell you now that the oath that I swore was an empty one, because I did undertake a difficult task.

It happened one morning during the harmattan season, when I woke up late. I hasten to say that ever since I became rich I had taken to waking up late because thinking too much kept me awake most of the night. Ever since I had returned from my second hunting expedition and women in the town realized I was rich, they had flocked to my house in droves. Of course I fell in love with them, and many of them became my wives, though in the main they married me more for my wealth than my character. They were not above saying, "Our interest lies in a man's wealth, and not in his nature; so even if he attacks us with his gun or hits us with his hunting bag, we will still marry him."

As soon as they became acquainted with my hunting habits, and noticed that a ruthless temperament had become integral to my character as a result of my dealings with elves and wild animals in the forest, they began to desert me, one by one. It happened that on the morning I just mentioned. I was now down to just nine wives. I was in conversation with one of them when the difficult task that I was about to undertake manifested itself as follows.

One of the King's messengers came in unexpectedly to tell me that the King would like to see me. This surprised me, but nevertheless I got up, put on my long, loose traditional garment, a pair of baggy shorts and a floppy hat, and went to visit the King in his palace.

The King received me with a smile, and said, "Akara-Ogun."

"Your Majesty," I replied, "I am he; may God grant you long life."

He called me a second time, saying, "Akara-Ogun."

I replied again, saying, "Long may you live; we are all your obedient servants."

He called me a third time: "Akara-Ogun."

I replied again, saying, "Your Majesty, that man stands before you. I am indeed Akara-Ogun, the exact embodiment of what the name I bear truly means. I am invulnerable to the evil forces of witches, wizards, and all malevolent beings."

The King burst out laughing, and said, "Then sit down at my right hand."

When I was sitting comfortably, the King turned to me and said, "My dear son, Akara-Ogun, I would like you to do something of great importance for me. But before I reveal the nature of my request, I wish to know if you are capable of carrying it out."

He had barely finished when I replied, "Your Majesty, this is a simple matter. The wind blows the grass wherever it pleases and a servant goes wherever his master sends him. Therefore, I am at your service, and you can despatch me in whatever direction you like, and I will surely go."

That promise was, of course, totally reckless, since it committed me to whatever the King demanded. He immediately began to address me as follows. "My son, do you realize that there is nothing in this world more important than good health? Do you also realize that there is nothing more honourable than to serve your country? These two things are far more important than gold and silver, and it is because of them that I must send you on the errand that I have mentioned. In this connection, before my father died he was fond of telling me a story about the King of a town which lay on the route through Irunmale Forest. The town was called Mount Langbodo, and he told me that the King had a particular gift which it was his habit to present to the brave hunters who visited his Kingdom. My father never told me exactly what this gift was, but he said that if any king could get hold of it, his kingdom would be very peaceful, and more famous than any other kingdom in the world. Therefore, since I know that you are a brave hunter, and internationally renowned for having been twice into the Forest of Daemons, I am delighted to call upon you today, and sincerely appeal to you to go to Mount Langbodo and get me this particular gift from the King."

I was naturally very frightened to hear this from the King, because I had often heard various stories about Mount Langbodo, and none of them mentioned anyone returning to recount his experiences there. In fact, before anyone could get there he would have to pass all the way through the Forest of Daemons, and only after that could the actual journey be said to have begun. The town itself cannot properly be regarded as belonging to this world, because it is in earshot of Heaven. You can imagine how reluctant I felt, but since I had mandated the King to send me wherever he pleased, I had no option but to honour my promise. I therefore replied to him as follows.

"Your Majesty, you are our father. The elders were right when they said, 'whatever experience the young may claim to possess, old age and the ravages of time still teach many things!' Your worship, I now realize that, despite all my experiences, I am still not as wise as you. You have out-witted me in this matter, and since I have given you my word of honour, I shall have to go, whether I like it or not. Well, that's of no importance; after all, it is for the benefit of my country that I must go. I would, therefore, like to ask a favour; I want you to send a town crier all through the town, to summon other brave hunters like myself to accompany me to this place, so that I will not have to die alone. Furthermore, I would also like you to send for other brave hunters from the neighbouring towns to accompany us on this historic journey to Mount Langbodo. Once you have done this everything should be satisfactory, and we will be ready to go."

The King was happy to fall in with my suggestions, and immediately ordered that my requests be carried out. By the third day, the hunters had all assembled at the palace, but when I inspected them I failed to see a man called Kako, whom I felt should definitely be included in this important expedition, because he was so strong. This is his story.

His mother was an elf and his father a goblin, but when he was born, Kako's complexion and other physical qualities were those of a human being. His parents, both being of elvish appearance, therefore rejected and abandoned him in a large hole in a tree of the kind called Ako, or ironwood. It happened that a passing hunter found him and took him home. He brought him up as his own son and named him Kako because he had been found in the ironwood tree. When I was young we used to play together and that was when I realized what sort of person he would be. At the age of twelve he killed a fully grown tiger with a cutlass, but told nobody about it. Only when the tiger had completely decomposed did he return to remove its femur, which he thereafter wielded as a cudgel, and was known as Kako, the Keeper of the Tiger-Cudgel.

Unfortunately, his step-father died soon after my own father's death, and indeed, the circumstances of our lives included some odd coincidences. Like me, he had also gone on an adventure into a forest near our town, which is known as the Great Forest, at about the same time that I first went into the Forest of Daemons at Irunmale. The Great Forest is just as terrible in its way, with more wild animals but fewer elves. Nevertheless, Kako was still in the Great Forest when we were planning our expedition to Mount Langbodo, so I went there to look for him.

I didn't arrive at the Great Forest that day, since I had left home a little late and stopped to sleep at nightfall, but I met Kako at about ten o'clock the following morning. When I saw him, I hardly recognized him as he had draped his body with palm leaves. I hadn't known that he was getting married to an elf that day. When he saw me he got up from where he was sitting and rushed to embrace me. We were very happy to see each other, and he told me of his experiences in the Great Forest. He had heard about my own extraordinary experiences in the Forest of Daemons and told me many things which I have not time to mention now, for if I were to recount them all, there would certainly be enough to fill a book.

After he had finished talking I told him all about my own demanding experiences, and when I had finished, we embraced once again to express our warm affection and joy at the meeting, for such is the custom when two supermen meet.

During the reminiscences I had not forgotten why I had come there, and once they were over, I said, "Kako, Keeper of the Tiger-Cudgel, my childhood friend, may I share a proverb with you?"

He replied, "My dear Akara-Ogun, please go ahead, I am listening."

I carried on as follows. "Did you know that as long as there is life, there will always be a reason to be engaged in doing something."

"That is certainly true," said Kako.

"Then, Kako, we should never give up trying until we have overcome all our problems – we still have much to do to improve the standing of our country in this world. However, there are reasons behind all things; and had the matter not been important, you would not have seen me here so unexpectedly. I am here because there is a group of minor hunters getting ready to mount a challenging expedition to Mount Langbodo for the good of our country, and after thinking long and hard about this matter, I became convinced that we should go with them. Moreover, should we hang back we would shame ourselves. It would be said that we were selfish, and without consideration for the good of our country. It is not good to forget about our country, because wherever we may go, be it to the east or the west, and however long our journeys may last, and however deep our love of adventure may be, we must still return to our own roots in the end. There is no place like home, and we must certainly go back there. Think on this, my friend!"

To cut a long story short, Kako packed his belongings and came away from the Great Forest with me.

It is the custom among the elves of the Great Forest that men and women must live together for a period of seven years before they marry. During this period they may naturally have children, and they also get to know each other very well. Only if they still find each other compatible after all this time do they get married as is their marriage contract dictates. Should they find themselves incompatible, they part peacefully by mutual consent and both the man and the woman immediately start looking for other partners. Kako was going through one of the customary rituals when I saw him draped in palm leaves for his wedding day, from which it follows that he and his wife had been living together for seven years when we met.

However, it may surprise you to learn that Kako did not inform his wife before he decided to come with me then and there. That was very irresponsible on his part, and when she learned that he had left, she quickly caught up with us and took hold of him, speaking as follows.

"What is the matter, my darling? What have I done wrong? What is my offence and how have I offended? Did you find me with another man? Have I been discourteous? Have I been lazy? Have I ever failed to prepare you meals on time? Have I ever failed to express my deep love and affection? Have you ever seen me quarrelling in public? Have I taken part in irresponsible gossip? Have I ever been extravagant? Have I ever behaved unreasonably? Have you found me unclean? Have I ever flouted your authority? Have I ever been disobedient, or failed in my duties as a housewife? Have I treated visitors casually? Have I failed in my duty of care towards you, or failed to understand your requirements? What can have caused this? Tell me, please tell me, for God's sake tell me, my darling, my husband, my sweetheart!"

"Yes," Kako replied, "it's true that any woman who understands all the things you have mentioned will never offend her husband, and I can honestly say you have never offended me, not even by taking too long over preparing my meals, an offence of which thousands of women are guilty every hour of every day. But no one can guard against the unexpected, when it arises. Nature works according to a predetermined time-scale, and every moment brings another experience. 'To everything, there is a season.' There is a time to play, a time to fight; a time to weep and a time for joy. Now is the time for me to leave, and I must definitely go. Therefore, you get about your business, and I will be with mine. If you find another suitor, I advise you to marry him. Please don't rely on me any more for I am going back home – Goodbye!"

When Kako had finished, the woman burst into tears and pleaded with him to stay, but he took no notice. Instead he picked up his cudgel, sheathed his sword and walked quickly away, like an office clerk in the rush-hour. When the woman realized that the situation was beyond repair, she began to lament, as follows.

"Alas! See what you have done to me! When you first offered to marry me I turned you down, but by your boasts you deceived me into believing that you were unlike other men, and I gave you my love. I was head-over-heels in love with you, so madly in love that I could do nothing without thinking of you. I could neither eat, nor drink, nor enjoy the society of friends if you were not there. Your voice was an irresistible pleasure to me. Though I was overwhelmed with your love and could bear it no longer, yet I sought ever to come closer to you, so that I could draw your attention to me. You knew that, except for you, I had no parents, no sister or brother. How I lament that you are suddenly leaving me now, just as our relationship was beginning to blossom! Do you want the elves to make a mockery of me, saying, 'When you knew what you were doing, why did you do it?' Ah, God will punish you, destroyer that you are!" After she had finished she took a firm hold of Kako, and said, "You are going nowhere today unless you do something about me."

After he heard her protestation, filled with anguish and anger in equal measure, Kako felt sorrow and regret, but he felt that he could not reveal these emotions before her. Nevertheless, when the woman had clung onto him for a long time and was, obviously, not about to let go of him, his attitude changed. He drew out his sword and said to her: "Do not be so stubborn, you witch, do not be such a stumbling-block to me; haven't you realized that before a wicked person is condemned to death, many good things would have been destroyed. It is also clear to me that before God passes his judgement on me, I should have to pass my own judgement on you. As soon as he finished speaking, he stabbed her through the stomach. The woman fell to the ground, writhing in pain and screaming Kako's name until she bled to death. It was a most harrowing sight.

We continued on our journey home, and on that day, we both slept in my father's house as Kako had no other house to go to. On the following morning, I went to tell the King that it was time to set a date for our journey, and we agreed to leave on the ninth day.

Kako and I both greatly enjoyed those nine days together because many of our friends, some of whom had been living in remote villages for years, had come home. We visited each other and went drinking palm wine. When, on these social occasions, the topic of the relationship between Kako and his jilted wife came up in conversation, we teased him for having taken up with such a resolutely and ruthlessly stubborn woman but Kako remained silent.

Thus the time passed quickly and Kako and I had packed our baggage by the evening of the eighth day. On the following morning, we made ourselves a breakfast of pounded yam, and by half-past eight we were on our way to the King's palace. We arrived to find him already sitting in majesty on his throne, with everyone from the town assembled before him. They arrived in droves, like locusts swarming on a farm. Many hunters had still to arrive when we got there, but they were all present by ten o'clock.

My dear friends, seeing is believing. You would really have had to be there to believe the sight, for even the townsfolk were bewildered, so impressive did the hunters appear. They were all sturdy upright men wearing their hunting clothes and with their hunting bags and sheathed swords hanging over their shoulders. Some were dressed in loose shorts, others wore only loincloths, but all had treated their guns with magic charms which made them turn black.

I can't give you all their names, but I can give you a brief description of six of the bravest and most famous. That means there were seven hunters of the highest rank, myself included, lined up before the King. The first in line was Kako, Keeper of the Tiger-Cudgel, whose history I have already told you. The second was Imodoye, whose name means 'Wisdom', my maternal cousin. When he was about ten he had been carried away by a whirlwind fairy, who kept him with her for seven years. Throughout that time she fed him one seed of alligator pepper every day. He was very wise and equally experienced as a medicine man and a hunter. It was from his sound judgement that he got his name which means wise and knowledgeable. I was third in line.

The fourth was Olohun-iyo [Soprano], the handsomest man in the world, and the best singer and drummer anywhere. At his drumbeat, a pall of smoke rises into the air, and the sound of his singing sends a wave of fire from his mouth. He specializes in musical and magical chants. The fifth was Elegbede-Ode, which means 'Superhuman Freak'. Although he was technically human, he had grown up among animals. This was because he had been born with three eyes – two in front and one at the back of his head. His birth had terrified his mother, for to bear a baby with three eyes was a most untoward event. She therefore abandoned him in the forest, where he grew up among gorillas and became very strong. At one period of his life, he had moved into town and taken up residence in the palace, but he retained the manners and outlook of a wild gorilla, which is how he acquired his nickname, Elegbede being the father of all gorillas. He lived with the King for a long time, and it was the King who bought him a gun so that he could become a hunter. He had a special talent for communicating with birds and animals, and was stronger than a lion – so strong as to be invulnerable to any physical assault or pain.

Oluhun-Iyo (Soprano)

The sixth hunter was Efoiye, the Archer. He was a foreigner whom I had never seen before the question of the expedition to Mount Langbodo came up. He was an archer, as his name implies, and he obviously belonged to the family of the birds, for he grew, downy feathers on his body instead of hair like a normal human being. He was always plucking himself, to avoid embarrassment. He also had feathers on his arms, and could fly, but no one could see them when he was fully clothed, as he only ever did that if he got into difficulties while hunting. Any arrow of Efoiye's would go wherever he wished – he didn't even have to see his target, as long as he instructed his arrow to go there, it would unfailingly find its way. But he was not allowed to use more than seven arrows in any one day, lest he offend Sokoti, the Smith of Heaven, who had given the arrows to Efoiye's father.

The seventh hunter was Aramada-Okunrin, whose name means 'Antipathy', and a cousin of Efoiye's on his father's side. He was an extraordinary man in that he had a negative reaction to the effects of the sun or any other heat, the hotter it got, the colder he felt. Contrariwise, if it turned cold he always felt hot, as things worked in reverse for him.

These were the seven who would be undertaking this important journey. Once we were all in position, the King gave us some useful advice, and when he had finished, Imodoye addressed the community as follows:

"Dear citizens, thank you for coming to see us today. You have responded as one would expect reasonable people to respond, and have demonstrated to us that you are responsible citizens. You have not only encouraged us, and made us feel confident, you have also made us positively look forward to setting forth on this journey. I would like to remind you therefore, that every effect has its cause; thus, had there been no good reason for it, you would never have seen us gathered here so unexpectedly. As you know, every one of us standing here before you is going to Mount Langbodo, and that is certainly in the national interest. But I would like you to bear in mind that however pleasant a sojourn may be, a guest will always look forward to coming home, and however much we may enjoy staying abroad, the thought of home will always be in our hearts. We should always be proud of our native land, even if it is as small as a bird's nest. We should always take pride in our country, even if it is a filthy rubbish heap, or the backward place of an uncivilized citizenry.

"The citizens of a country are its builders and architects, who can shape it to reflect their taste. They can make a filthy country clean, and a small one great, but anyone who renounces his native land is stupid. From my own wealth of knowledge and long experience, I can see that the journey which we are about to undertake is dangerous. At times we will face formidable hazards; we will suffer hardship and distress. Above all, we are unsure of returning home in the same condition as we set out. Many of us may never see this country again, but we hope you will not forget us when we are gone. Finally, I thank you all on behalf of my comrades, who are also honoured to take journey to Mount Langbodo – farewell, and God be with you! We are leaving behind our friends and acquaintances, our relatives, homes, and belongings are in your care. We sincerely hope that you will look after them on our behalf. If we return, well and good; if we never meet again in this life, may we meet in Heaven!"

When he had finished this speech all the women burst into tears, and the men looked sad and depressed, but he turned to us and said: "My dear comrades who are now going to Mount Langbodo, take courage and be strong! I ask you, where is the pride of a man who takes pleasure in an easy life, and renders no service to his country? What honour has a lazy man, compared to a brave man? A lazy man is worthless compared to a brave man, and any reputation he gathers will soon fade. Why, I ask, are you looking so sad? I would like to remind you that Sodeke played a remarkable role among the Egbas before he died; Ogedengbe did the same among the Ijeshas, and Ogunmola did likewise among the Yorubas before he, too, died. Therefore, I ask you again, are we or are we not going to play a magnificent role?"

Imodoye was most impressive as he delivered this speech, which instilled confidence into us all. We said, unanimously, "We will definitely play our parts; come, let us go."

Thus we set out on our journey, and all the people followed us as far as the border, before returning home in tears, but when they had all gone there was still one old man following us. After he had walked a short distance with us alone, he asked us to stop and spoke to us as follows:

"Gentlemen, as you proceed on this journey, try to avoid any dissension or ill-will among yourselves. Remember that it takes both hands to lift a load to the head, and five fingers to put food in the mouth. Many hands make light work, and bring a quick conclusion. Therefore, in the difficult times ahead, you will need to cooperate together as a team. From now on, I advise you not to think of your homes. The trail should be your guide, so concentrate your minds on where you are going. If wild animals attack you, be prepared to defend yourselves against them; if evil spirits trouble you, defy them; and whenever you are on your own, constantly review your plans. Follow my advice, and you will benefit; but if you reject it, there will come a time when you say to yourselves, 'Alas! We were warned by the old man!'" Having said this, he returned home in tears.

I cannot tell you all the events that we experienced before we completed our journey through the Forest of Daemons at Irunmale, though I may do so at some later date if I have time. Nevertheless, I must briefly mention something relating to my friend the King whom I spoke of yesterday, in whose Kingdom I killed the one-eyed tiger. We passed through his Kingdom on the way to Mount Langbodo, and he received us and looked after us very well, providing a plentiful feast and replenishing our supplies of food for the journey. He told me that the dog which I had been accused of stealing was still alive, and that my enemies had hidden it somewhere so that I would be held responsible for its loss.

The brave hunters to Mount Langbodo

After leaving the forest behind, we had a strange experience. We suddenly found ourselves enclosed on all sides by dense vegetation and could see no way ahead to Mount Langbodo. We had no space to turn round because the vegetation was like a solid stockade and I doubt that even a mouse could have found a way through it. We tried to hack our way through it, but the more we cut, the quicker it grew back. In the end we gave up and resigned ourselves to death, as we felt nothing worse could befall us, but on the third night of our confinement on that spot, we saw two big birds alight on a nearby tree.

Instinctively Kako picked up his gun to shoot them, but Elegbede-Ode signalled to him not to do so, though soon afterwards he himself shot one of them dead. I remind you that he could communicate with birds and he had signalled Kako to hold fire because he could overhear what the birds were saying to each other. In fact, the bird he shot dead was telling the other bird that Kako had got us into trouble that time in the Great Forest by causing the death of the innocent jilted woman who was still calling his name as she lay dying on the ground. The bird also observed, smugly, that unless we killed it as a sacrifice, to atone for Kako's terrible offence, God would never be pleased with us, and never release us from our imprisonment. That is why Elegbede-Ode killed it.

According to traditional ritual, we cut open the bird's stomach and poured some palm oil into it. Then we put it in a small potsherd and left it by a large tree, not far from there. God was happy that we repented, not because of our sacrifice, but because He realised that if we had been wiser we would have worshipped Him better.

A little while later I had a sudden inspiration; I remembered the woman who had rescued me from Agbako's imprisonment. As you will recall, I encountered Agbako (Calamity), the sixteen-eyed monster during my first visit to the Forest of Daemons where we had an epic fight after which he imprisoned me underground. So I got some incense out of my bag and made a fire to burn it. I called upon her to rise from the earth as I performed a hunting ritual. Soon, she appeared from the ground in the distance, and I drew her to my comrade's attention: "Look, here comes the woman who rescued me from Agbako's imprisonment. Her name is Iranlowo, which means 'Help'."

When she got closer she said to me, "Here I am, Akara-Ogun, why have you summoned me?" I told her how we had been unable to get out of this place for the last three days, and how we had carried out the instruction that Elegbede-Ode had overheard in the conversation of the birds, and that I had called upon her to rise from within the earth to help set us free from our imprisonment.

Iranlowo listened carefully to what I had to say, and as soon as I had finished she asked us to follow her, which we did. The thick vegetation surrounding us parted before her as we advanced, and soon we were once again on the road to Mount Langbodo. There she left us to resume our adventure.

We had not gone far when it began to get dark, so we made camp, and set forth early next morning after we were woken by the cooing of a cuckoo trumpeting its song. We had no trouble until about half past ten when we saw a man in the distance whose name we knew to be Eru, which means 'Fear'.

We were naturally terrified when we saw Eru, for he had four heads. Only one was a human head, and it faced east; the second was like that of a lion, and faced west; the third was that of a big snake dripping venom from its tongue, and faced south, while the north-facing head was that of a poisonous fish, from whose mouth streamed a mighty fire. Various snakes coiled around his neck, innumerable scorpions clung to his shoulder, and his entire body was covered in hair. Swarms of honey-bees and wasps buzzed round him, and he kept swatting them with his hands as he walked along. A gust of wind preceded him, heralding his arrival, and carrying a vibrant sound through the forest. Both the timber trees and the palm trees rattled with it, making a warning noise which formed these words: "Eru is sent unto the disobedient, as the avenging agent of God, to rid the world of undesirables so that they will pollute it no longer!" Indeed, this man symbolized great terror, and when he saw us, he stopped to inspect us. Kako and Elegbede-Ode stepped forward to fight him but though they tried several times they could not get close as they were forced back by the honey bees and wasps. Then Efoiye shot at him with his arrows, but they had no effect. After that, we all applied our various magical skills, but without success.

Finally Imodoye asked Olohun-iyo to serenade a song of lamentation. He warned him to sing nothing likely to inspire smoke or fire, but instead a sentimental melody with emotional appeal that might influence Eru to show us some compassion. Olohun-iyo began to serenade as Imodoye had suggested. The words were about how God had created the Heaven and the Earth, and about how he had so loved humankind that he had visited them as a friend. The lyric also related how it was the sins of the people which had discouraged God from visiting them, but that the people now recognized the evil of their sins, and had begun to refrain from committing them. It further stressed that anyone who hindered others in their pursuit of virtue should be regarded as the greatest sinner of all, of whom God had said that it would be best to tie a granite millstone round the neck of such a sinner and cast him into the depths of the sea. The climax of his song covered the nature of our journey, which was to serve the interests of our country, and which had brought us the highest favour of God. It also highlighted our recent, almost unprecedented, unpleasant experiences, from which only God could save us should we ever experience anything similar.

At regular intervals he embellished his song with magical incantation, so that after a while Eru took to his heels and disappeared from view. Thus did we use mere song to dispose of the man for whom neither gun nor arrow could harm. Thus we achieved by patience what physical force could not.

We resumed our journey, walking until it was getting dark and we could hear a woodcock singing. When we found a suitable place we stopped, and everyone lay down to sleep wherever was most convenient. Next morning we gave thanks to God that we had woken up safe and sound, and went on our way.

At exactly half-past seven in the morning we arrived at a town, and were about to go in when we saw a notice inscribed on the border gates. It read:

> In the name of Ostrich, the Patriarch of Birds,
> the undisputed King of Birds:

> God does not object to the killing of birds for food.
> God does not object to birds being used for good purposes.
> But anyone who has, at any time, killed any bird for
> no good reason, is excluded from our Kingdom.
> No unjustified person may enter our Kingdom.

This was without doubt, the Kingdom of the Birds, where Ostrich held sway. If any visitor had killed or mistreated any bird without good reason, then the moment he entered that town, a round red blotch like a bloodstain would suddenly appear as a halo in front of him, though he would not be aware of it. We had expected none of this when we first arrived, nevertheless, we had all thrown stones at birds when we were young and must have killed some without good reason at some time in our lives.

In fact the mysterious red halo appeared in front of every one of us, and none of us was aware of it until the police arrested us and took us before Ostrich. This Ostrich was quite unlike the ordinary domestic ostrich which is so common in people's homes. From the neck down to the feet he looked like a bird, but his head was a human head of the usual size, though bald and shiny at the crown, and his neck was longer and thinner than that of a common, domestic ostrich. In his normal sitting posture his long neck coiled round and round in a spiral loop, with his shiny head sticking out in front.

On seeing us he addressed us angrily, saying, "Who are you? Where are you from? Where are you going? You are most certainly villains, and the evidence of that is clear on every one of you. Therefore, prepare yourselves quickly, because today I am going to deal with you rigorously. You shall do three things for me, and if you fail, I will kill the lot of you!"

This greatly enraged Kako, who was about to offer a contemptuous answer when Imodoye restrained him. Imodoye then replied to Ostrich in these terms.

"We have not come here to steal, nor to do harm to anyone. We are only travelling to Mount Langbodo. Therefore, if there is any service that you require of us, we will definitely perform it, for we seek no quarrel with you, and desire to be your friends."

At that, the King calmed down, but he nonetheless told us that our first task was to select someone from our group whose task would be to give battle to a great wild beast which lived in his father's shrine. According to his description, the beast was built like a lizard but four times the size of a grown man, and bore on his head, a central horn about two feet long as strong as steel and sharply pointed. When the beast hunted for food, it used the horn to stab its prey and had never been known to miss. The King only needed to visit the shrine once a year where he would see the beast, and needed magical protection before he looked at it.

As you all know, Kako had acquired unmatched experience hunting in the Great Forest, so when he heard this demand, Kako immediately astonished the Ostrich King by volunteering to go and fight the beast. In fact, this courageous gesture quite saddened the King because Kako was a handsome man, sturdy, upright and taller than any of us. Nevertheless, when Ostrich realized that Kako was determined to go, he let him with the hope and intention that he would be killed. We were frightened by Kako's courageous act and followed him weeping.

Once we reached and entered the shrine, Ostrich took us to a big orchard, with many different kinds of fruit trees. Directly in front of us there was a narrow path leading straight into a small mausoleum about two minutes away, where the beast was supposed to lurk. As this particular beast could talk like a man, the King had sent a message ahead of us that he was bringing someone for him to slaughter for food.

The beast came out of the mausoleum as soon as he received the message, and when we saw him approaching, we all ran away including the King. But Kako stayed put, leaning casually against a tree. The beast saw him, and crept towards him. Just before he reached Kako, the beast leapt with great force, intending to impale him on its pointed horn, but Kako dodged just in time. The beast missed, and ran its horn deep into a tree instead. Kako was very happy to see this, but instead of taking the opportunity to stab it with his sword, he picked up a big stone and started to beat the beast on the head with it in order to drive its horn deeper into the tree. Once it was well stuck, he drew out his cudgel and clubbed the beast to death.

Thus did Kako kill the terrible beast, and when he came out of the shrine, people and animals alike were terrified; yet Ostrich greeted and congratulated him. The first task had been accomplished, but the second was now imminent. Ostrich, in his capacity as King of the birds, called Imodoye and asked him to tell us that one of us must make ready to fight the gnomes. As we all knew, the gnomes lived in an underground cavern, and none was taller than a foot. Every one of them carried a small stick wherever he went, and they existed in huge numbers.

Imodoye had hardly finished passing on the King's message when, once again, Kako volunteered to fight, this time with the gnomes. All the rest of us had declined this challenge, but he insisted.

As the rest of us were deliberating over this matter among ourselves, our guardian lady, Iranlowo (Help) who had rescued me from Agbako, reappeared, carrying a bag. She told us to let Kako go and we all agreed.

Ogongo (Ostri
the King of Bir

Once this was approved, she gave him a bag filled with special sand and instructed him to throw a scoop of the sand at the gnomes as soon as they arrived. She added that if he did as she told him, the gnomes would go blind and lash out, killing one another. She then explained that the sand came from the border of Heaven and had been especially created by God to blind anyone who attempted to hinder others from the commission of worthy acts. The woman also warned Kako not to carry his cudgel with him, but he ignored that warning. We all joined in her warning, but he refused to listen, and said: "A snail and its shell are an inseparable whole, just as my cudgel and I are inseparable." As time was by then running out, Imodoye requested us to say no more, and leave Kako alone with his cudgel. He then sent word to the King that we were ready.

Ostrich was surprised to see that we had chosen Kako again, and was certain that he would die in this encounter. He led Kako out of town, the rest of us following, and after a while we came to an open clearing in the forest. It was sandy, without vegetation, and about a square mile in area. There Ostrich sacrificed a cow to appease the gnomes, and Imodoye sacrificed a pigeon, which symbolizes all things worthy of honour, and a dove, which symbolizes all things worthy of peace, grace and dignity. He also spoke a few words of supplication thus: "As honour benefits the nature of pigeons; peace and comfort befit the nature of doves; therefore, may today be a day of honour for Kako!"

As soon as Imodoye had completed this symbolic ritual, Ostrich threw a measure of water before him and began to recite some incantations. After he had been doing this for a while, we saw a multitude of gnomes approaching from the distance – a frightening sight for all of us. Kako prepared himself to confront them, and when they saw him, they came running towards him.

Soon they descended upon Kako like a swarm of locusts invading a small cornfield; they surrounded him, and attacked him like a thousand ants over crumbs of food. I am sorry to say that Kako had forgotten his instructions, and on the impulse of the moment drew his cudgel to club the gnomes to death. Within minutes he had killed fifty of them, but this had an insignificant effect on so great an army of gnomes. They overwhelmed him by sheer numbers, so that we could no longer see him. They rained painful blows on Kako, and after this had been going on for some time Iranlowo asked Olohun-iyo to start singing and beating his drum to remind Kako of what he was supposed to do.

As Olohun-iyo began, fire broke out and the whole area was engulfed in smoke. At that moment, every one of us, including the King and the gnomes, forgot about the fight and began to dance. While we were dancing, Kako got the sense of Olohun-iyo's words. He immediately took a handful of sand from the bag and threw it at the gnomes who were all struck blind at once. Once this had happened, Iranlowo asked Olohun-iyo to stop drumming. The gnomes then began to fight among themselves until all were dead except one, whom Kako clubbed to death with his cudgel. Thus did we accomplish the second task set us by King Ostrich.

But before we could leave the Kingdom of the Birds, the Ostrich King told us to carry out the third task. He told us that there was a man named Were-orun, which means 'Celestial Lunatic', who was so wicked that God felt obliged to expel him from heaven and send him to the bird's Kingdom. God hoped that listening to beautiful bird songs might make a better person of him, but the birds, instead of singing their beautiful songs which might indeed have had that effect, set Were-orun difficult tasks to perform. For example, if there was any creature that the birds wanted killed, all they had to do was summon Were-orun from his den and offer the creature to him. He would immediately kill it, regardless of whether it was a human being, a bird, an animal or an elf.

Coincidentally, the wicked man's den was not far from where we were, and when Kako said that he was still game for a fight, we let him please himself. When we had all got to the den, Ostrich called for him to come out. While he was on his way, the whole place started to shake. There was a clap of thunder and a pall of dust covered the sky. We were all quaking with fear and I barely retained control of my bowels! When Were-orun finally appeared in the distance, his eyes were incandescent like balls of red fire, and his breath was like a very hot steam.

As he advanced towards us, Kako went to meet him, and once they met they began to fight. Were-orun's intention was to tear Kako to pieces within a minute, but that was not as simple as he anticipated as Kako had the same intentions towards him. As they fought, dust again filled the sky until we could no longer see them clearly. Unfortunately, a full account of this fight cannot be included here because it would take too long; but at one point Were-orun lost his temper for he had never encountered anyone like Kako before. He spat on his hand, and after reciting some incantations, rubbed the spittle on his head. That set his body ablaze, and Kako had to step back from him because he could no longer hold on to him. This annoyed Elegbede-ode and he, together with Aramada-okunrin, attacked Were-ogun. After they had been fighting for a while, Elegbede-ode could no longer stand the effects of the heat coming from Were-orun, and had to withdraw; but Aramada-okunrin was unaffected by the heat because of his contrary nature. In fact, as he went on with the fight, he was feeling colder and colder. After a while, the fire became so fierce that we could hardly see them at all – they were so covered in the fire which continued to burn for about two hours before it finally went out. When it did, we saw Aramada-okunrin sitting on Were-orun's corpse. He said to us, laughing, "I have killed him – come and have a look. I don't even feel that I've been fighting, except that I am feeling a bit cold."

Thus did we accomplish all the three tasks which we had been set by King Ostrich on behalf of all the birds.

Now that we had completed all the tasks, the King invited us to dinner, and had a great feast prepared for us.

Every one of us ate to full repletion, which meant that Kako ate enough for six grown men and drank about a keg of palm wine. When he was well drunk and quite out of his mind, he moved closer to the King and patted him on the head, saying, "Your bald head is shiny!" The birds were greatly offended at this loutish conduct and set upon us. The scuffle reached a point where I became concerned that they were both stronger and outnumbered us, so I took one of the alligator pepper pods which the elf had given me some time ago, and broke it into pieces. After I had taken out all the seeds, I gave one each to my comrades and swallowed one myself.

All at once feathered wings began to grow from our arms which enabled us to fly into the sky to escape the attack of the birds. But they pursued us there where a serious fight developed – so serious, indeed, that both Kako's brother Janduku (whose name meant 'Ruffian') and Imodoye's brother Ojuri (whose name meant ' Experience') were killed. Nevertheless we defeated the birds in the end and continued flying towards Mount Langbodo. After we had flown for some distance, Kako suggested that we should go back to walking as to continue flying might be interpreted as a sign of cowardice on our part. We all agreed with him so I gave everyone another alligator pepper seed from a different pod. When we had all eaten them, the wings on our arms retracted and we resumed our journey on foot.

Soon we arrived at an animal kingdom where we experienced many difficulties. Although I can't go into detail about this, I can tell you that I lost one bicuspid tooth there. I have been unable to chew my food properly since then because of the gap it has left in my mouth.

After we left the animal kingdom we went through 'Hell and High Seas', as the expression goes. We passed through one town where every man had twelve arms and met with seven scolding women who had the ill-temper of vixens and who cried all the time. It would be wearisome to recall and recount all our countless experiences in these places so it easier to say nothing.

We continued on our journey until we had reached the top of a hill. From there we saw Agbako, the notorious sixteen-eyed freak-monster, in the distance, coming towards us up on the other side. As soon as I saw him I shouted, "We're in trouble!" When my comrades asked me why I shouted like that, I gave them the reason, but Kako and the other brave hunters were angry. However, before Agbako could get close to us, Efoiye shot him with an arrow. Although the arrow found him, it did no harm. Efoiye shot him twice more, but still with no effect, and Agbako continued climbing towards us until Efoiye had shot all the seven arrows he was permitted. Just before Agbako reached us, heading directly for Efoiye, he shot an eighth arrow, having forgotten that he was allowed no more than seven in a day. This so greatly angered Sokoti, the Smith of Heaven, that he endowed Agbako with supernatural strength from Heaven, which caused us great confusion. At that point I called upon God, and he responded. Agbako quickly collapsed on the ground where he transformed himself into a snake and coiled round Kako. The snake tripped Kako and they both went tumbling down the hill. When they reached level ground at the bottom, Agbako transformed himself back into an elf. Then Kako lifted him off the ground and threw him down with all his strength. This killed him, and we continued our journey.

We experienced so many difficulties that it would take me too long to describe them all, but I will mention just one more incident. It happened one morning while we were walking that we suddenly noticed a man approaching us from behind. His name was Egbin, which means 'Filth', and we could smell him from miles away, long before we could see him. My dear friends, I must confess I have never encountered such a disgusting creature since I was born. All his toes were infested with jiggers, so many that the ends of some toes had dropped off. They also infested his legs from sole to knee, to such an extent that they wriggled and dropped out as he walked. There were sores of various sizes on his legs, which he covered with leaves, the smallest being about the size of my palm, though some of the sores were left uncovered as the leaves were not large enough. All these festering sores oozed pus and other morbid fluids as he moved.

Such was Egbin's lack of basic personal hygiene that there was three years' worth of dried excrement round his anus, and whenever he paused to rest, worms and mobile piles wriggled out of his backside and crawled all over him while he kept pulling them away from himself. He emptied his bowels without removing his trousers wherever and whenever he felt inclined, so that the discharged faeces smeared his thighs and legs as he went. He also had a great variety of boils and blisters all over his body, each bigger than my fist. When they burst, he dipped his fingers into the copious flow of pus that they discharged onto his body and licked them.

Egbin never bathed – never in his life. The sticky matter oozing from the comers of his eyes was like a creamy vomit, and the stench that arose was like that of rotten meat that is infested with maggots. His neck was rough and scaly like the skin of a toad, and covered by thick layers of dirt which made it quite black. Earthworms, snakes, scorpions and all sorts of creeping creatures crawled in and out of his mouth when he talked, and they provided his food whenever he was hungry. Egbin's nose never ceased to drip mucus, and that was what he used as cooking water for his food, and for drinking water as well. Those, my dear friends, are the few details that I can remember about this tramp.

When he got near to us he laughed, showing off the creamy matter that coated his teeth, and we asked him to go away. After a while he did, but a man called Oto, which means 'Difference' and was a brother of Aramada-okunrin followed him, and had not been seen or heard of since.

About three days after this, we came to a road which led straight to Heaven, and was within earshot of it. There we met two handsome youths in white robes. They greeted us cordially, and asked us where we were going. We told them that we were going to Mount Langbodo. They were very pleased, and gave us directions, saying that the road on which we had been trekking was the same as the road leading to Heaven. They added that if we went on walking a little further, we would come to the road leading to Mount Langbodo on the right. On the border of the town, we would find a notice saying; 'This road leads to Mount Langbodo, the City of the Wise.' They added that if we kept on our present road without taking the turning to Mount Langbodo, we would find that it divided at the top, leading to two separate destinations. The right hand fork would lead us to Heaven, the left would lead us to Hell. They also warned us to take care that we took the road to Mount Langbodo, because the division was not far from the earshot of Heaven itself. They stressed that if we failed to take due care we might stray onto the road leading to Heaven. That could cause us some serious problems, because the gatekeepers would prevent us from entering Heaven in our current physical forms as human beings. We might then be killed by wild beasts, or even transformed into elves of the forest.

So they advised us, and we thanked them and walked on. After a short distance, we began to hear song from Heaven. To my regret, I have to tell you that I can find no adequate words to describe the beauty of that song to you. I had never heard such beauty before, and I greatly doubt that there can ever be a song like it in this world again. There were many people singing, but so perfect was their harmony that the effect was of a single voice, and the allure of the song was such that when we got to the junction leading to Mount Langbodo, we paused for a while and didn't want to take the turning. While we were still undecided what to do, a junior brother of Olohun-iyo's, called Keke-okun, which means 'Reel' or 'Spool', took the road to Heaven on his own. We warned him not to go, but he ignored us, and even while we were pleading with him not to go, many were tempted to follow his example. When Imodoye noticed our confusion he asked Olohun-iyo to start singing, so as to remind us of the purpose of our journey. He began to sing, and as his voice reached its crescendo it sent a wave of vibration throughout the forest and its environs. It was at that point that we recovered our sense of purpose and concentrated on pursuing our journey down the road to Mount Langbodo, but unfortunately we never found out what happened to Keke-okun. Some people say he was killed by wild beasts, others that he has been transformed into an elf, and still others say that the gatekeepers of heaven kindly kitted him out with immortal raiment so that he could enter into Heaven. But these are all mere speculations, since nobody knows what truly happened, and it's hard to know whom to believe. The one fact of which we are all convinced is that he set out there in our presence, and we did not witness his return before resuming our journey.

We trekked on for some considerable time, but it seemed we were not going to reach Mount Langbodo in daylight.

Once we were all feeling tired, and it was getting dark, we laid down our baggage to sleep some way off the path not realizing that we had little distance left to cover before reaching our destination. When we woke in the morning and looked in our bags, we realized that we had got no food left and feared we might starve before we reached our destination. We would have had no cause for concern on this score had I remembered to bring with me the scrap of cloth which my former fairy wife had given me at the time of my second visit to the Forest of Daemons, just before she left me to return to her home in the Bottomless Pit. But I had left it at home when we set out for Mount Langbodo. Had we had it with us and used it to ask for food, plenty would have been instantly provided, even here. But fortunately, we had only a short distance left to cover before we reached our destination.

I must tell you honestly that Mount Langbodo was a great city and beautiful beyond description. The roads were straight and wide, laid out in a grid and paved with brass. The walls of the houses were made of glass, the doors were silver and the window-frames were gold. The palace glowed beautifully in the low early morning sunshine, and the King sat in majesty on his throne, looking very beautiful with an oblong face.

Once we were in the city, we sent a message to the King who was glad to hear of our arrival. He ordered that we should be served with food and drink and attired in such beautiful clothes as would be suitable to wear when we were brought before him. His servants followed these instructions, and took us to meet the King. He welcomed us cordially, and we responded with courtesy, prostrating ourselves flat before him, and saying in chorus, "Your Majesty the King!"

Once we had completed our greeting in this friendly fashion, he promised to help us accomplish our mission to his Kingdom so that we could return home happily to our own King. But he insisted that before he could help us, we would have to spend seven days with Iragbeje in his house of seven bedrooms. However it must be said that this particular sage known as Iragbeje, was an extraordinary creature of great wisdom, having been endowed with exceptional intelligence from birth.

Ogodogo, whose name means 'Everlasting Glory' is the Potter of Heaven, whose business it is to sculpt all the babies that are born on Earth. He is always so pleased at the completion of each that he gives thanks to God, exclaiming, "The Glory of God is made manifest, and has become a living spirit in this child." He always says this, which is why the people in Heaven have given him his nickname. When he has finished sculpting the clay models of a batch of babies, he takes them to Sokoti, the Smith of Heaven, and together they fire the clay models in the kiln in Sokoti's smithy. After they have been fired they take the finished products to God.

At the very beginning of the world, after the creation of Adam and Eve our fore-parents, it was God's intention to give life to the clay models brought before Him and to ask them to put on one of the immortal outfits, which were kept (along with the mortal outfits) in Ogodogo's house. This would have given us all perpetual life on Earth, and our fore-parents might be alive even yet. There is no doubt that people would also have been more intelligent than they are. For example, we would have been able to understand the Egyptian pyramids, which our forebears built with stone, and all the other extraordinary works which bear witness to the great imagination of past times, and are still the great wonders of the world today. But unfortunately, the stubborn, animal nature of Mankind has deprived us of these most welcome benefits. The sins of our forebears forced God to change His mind and He commanded that all the babies born on Earth should wear mortal outfits instead so that life would be only a temporary experience for them.

However, when the wise sage Iragbeje was given his life and went to Ogodogo to try on an outfit, he arrived when Ogodogo was not at home, and instead of waiting until he returned, he went to where the outfits were kept and selected one of the immortal outfits which he put on quickly and then fled away into the world. Although God had not expected Iragbeje to behave in such a way according to His own pre-determined plan, the immortal out fits conferred power over life to such an extent that Iragbeje need never die because they are the same that God's supernatural beings wear in Heaven. Thus did Iragbeje become immortal, acquiring the wisdom of great experience and knowledge of the world. But after some time the world came to bore him so he went to live at Mount Langbodo where he applied his intelligence in various ways. There were seven rooms in his house which was thus called the "House of Seven Bedrooms" because he lived in one room for each day of the week, moving to the next in rotation. On the day we arrived the King sent him a message that we would be coming to spend seven days with him, but we spent our first night at Mount Langbodo in the palace.

CHAPTER 6

The First Day with Iragbeje in the House of Seven Bedrooms

On the second day of our arrival at Mount Langbodo, the King had his servants conduct us to Iragbeje. Once we were there, we were taken to a large room at the far end of the house. My dear comrades, I can tell you, it was a beautiful room! The floor was inlaid with precious stones which glittered like mirrors, and were as bright as the glittering torrent of a waterfall. When we first entered it, we thought the room must have been built over a stream, but it was the reflections from the precious stones that gave that impression. Ah! Iragbeje was a great man!

There were chairs of many different designs in this room, but they all glittered like lightning. Once we were all seated, Iragbeje took the highest chair, facing the rest, and addressed us.

"Hail brave hunters!" he began, "Welcome. It's a pleasure to greet you after your great trek. I rejoice in your safe arrival, and the fortitude and perseverance you have displayed in overcoming the challenges you have encountered throughout your journey. May I ask if you met Agbako on your way? I hope Egbin didn't pester you unnecessarily! How did you resolve the various problems you must have met on your way through the turbulent rivers? Did you find it necessary to fight in the Kingdom of the birds? I hope you suffered no harm at the hands of Were-orun? (Celestial lunatic) Did you meet any gnomes? How did you fare among the wild beasts? I commend your efforts and your cooperative team-spirit, as well as your individual courage, patience, endurance, self-confidence and determination. Once again, welcome, and well done!"

We responded cordially to this greeting, and once it was over, he continued with his address as follows. "I learnt about your arrival yesterday, and that you would be coming to spend seven days with me. So I have written down a programme of topics we will discuss during your seven day visit. According to my plan, today the subject will be children, who are the leaders of tomorrow, as the child of today is the father of tomorrow.

I therefore want every individual to listen carefully to my words, just as if I was talking to you personally, as individuals. This is my message.

"Dear young parent, begin to train your child while he is still young, and remember that he comes to you as a gift. Do not let your child grow up without a proper upbringing. In that way, you will not in the future suffer shameful regret at the sight of him becoming a social liability or depending for his sustenance on the generosity of others. Find him something worthwhile to do every morning so that he doesn't grow up lazy and useless. Do not let him have his own way all the time, give him moral guidance if and whenever he misbehaves, and bring him to order if he is ill-mannered. If you are wealthy, do not over-indulge your child. Do not encourage him to depend on the protection and services of other children; remember that over-indulgence and cossetting can ruin the life of a child from a wealthy home, so don't even let him realize that his family is wealthy. Do not let him grow up expecting to get whatever he asks for, and resist if he tries to persuade you to indulge him by applying improper pressure. Remember that nothing is forever in this world, and one day you yourself may be poor again – or even penniless. "On the other hand, if you are poor, try to live within such means as you have, and do not strive to emulate the rich, for that way you will never be free of debt. Everyone should live according to his means. "Moreover, whether you are rich or poor, you should be capable of exerting a certain degree of control over your wife, otherwise she may ruin your child's life by over-indulging him. While some wives take good care of their children, others ruin their lives because being women they are by nature too sentimental. Do not allow your child to mix in the sort of bad company where he would drink heavily from an early age, go about insulting women, and in general behaving irresponsibly while making such boasts as, 'We have no rivals! We are the champions! We rule OK?' Otherwise your child will become an outcast in polite society and stigmatized as a pathological alcoholic who gets drunk on plantain wine, drunk on raw spirits, drunk on palm wine by the keg, drunk on barley wine and, worst of all, gets drunk on borrowed money. Drunk, drunk, drunk!

"If you are forced by circumstances to place your child with foster-parents, make sure that you give him to responsible people, because many foster-parents lack adequate experience in looking after children. Do not entrust your child to very strict foster-parents who will ill-treat him, nor give him to woolly-minded liberals who will not be able to give him the discipline he needs or mould his mind appropriately. Moreover, it is inadvisable to allow either paternal or maternal grandmothers to foster children, so avoid that situation if you can. But if it becomes necessary for you to allow your child to be fostered by either of them on account of their obvious advantages of mutual help and company, well enough; do this if you please, but make sure you live sufficiently nearby so that you can keep an eye on him to prevent things from getting out of hand.

"Watch your child's language and make sure that he doesn't tell lies or indulge in silly gossip or the kind of irresponsible scandal mongering that can result in a person becoming a pathological criminal, trusted by no one, and certain to wind up in jail. If you can afford it, have your child educated; if you cannot, while living within your means, try to educate him yourself, even at the cost of some inconvenience. Be patient until you have accomplished your end, bearing in mind that one intelligent child is better than a thousand dull ones. Even so, while you are planning this endeavour, and before you embark on it, ensure that you are not going to give up halfway, lest people mock you, saying things like, 'Shame on you, shame on you; you promised to do things you were unable to fulfil. Shame on *you*!'

"Having to endure such insults will be trivial compared to what will follow, for your child's condition will be worse than it was before, as he will now be a half-educated person. Experience has shown that half-educated people feel ashamed to take work as a farm labourer, yet lack the educational background necessary to obtain a decent job. He may want to wear shoes, but hasn't the means to buy a loincloth! Therefore, if you know you cannot afford to give your child a complete education, you should not force yourself beyond your means – make sure instead that you give him the opportunity to learn a worthwhile trade. For example, you can encourage him to be a good farmer – we Africans are fortunate in having inherited vast areas of fertile land, a natural endowment which has descended from generation to generation. Alternatively, you can encourage your child to be a good businessman, or a carpenter; but whichever, do not give him the opportunity to half-learn a trade and then drop it, like a dilettante. You should realize that it is his time, and you must give him the opportunity and the help to make the most of it. You must not let yourself become annoyed with your child, saying such things as, 'I am not going to help him because his mother's behaviour has been undesirable, and he himself is useless.' I also want you to realize that however well-developed a child may be physically, his father cannot abandon his moral obligations as a father – they are lifelong. The experience of children is limited compared to their ability to learn. They may have acquired education, or a taste for fashionable or beautiful things, but these are nothing compared to the wealth of experience which the older generation has acquired, and which can never be diminished, however times change, or circumstances alter. Therefore, consider your plan carefully; give your child a good training now so that he can grow up to be a good citizen and never have reasons to curse you for neglecting your responsibilities – which could, moreover, cause you to die of a broken heart. Tell him this:

'Now it is your turn, young one, to receive from me some pieces of advice. Ah! Young one, don't you care for your mother? Or don't you think about her any more? Please, I appeal to you, don't behave like this, for you may bring unpleasant consequences upon yourself. Remember that when you were a helpless baby, it was your mother who cared for you, and kept you clean and tidy. You didn't only suck at her breast, you also fondled, pulled and bit it as you pleased. Moreover, while you were doing these things, you soiled her clothes with urine and faeces. Your father was responsible for finding and collecting the herbs needed to prepare your medicines, and both parents rallied round to give you the care you needed when you were sick. They were responsible for clothing and feeding you – and may I ask, what else did you need that they did not provide? Therefore it is important that you show your great appreciation in return. Make sure that you apply yourself seriously to complete the education and training that has been provided for you, so that you will be able to care for them and yourself out of the income you will earn by working at your occupation. You should not feel ill-treated if they lack sufficient means to educate you, nor envy those children whose parents can afford to educate them, because you should remember that as our fingers are not all equal, so neither are our destinies in life. Instead, apply yourself to advancement in your chosen occupation which is your only hope for a better future. Reflect that everybody is equally important, whether he is a farmer, a clerk or a trader, because as long as one works, there is every possibility of getting rich.

'Some children are reckless, irresponsible, unreliable and ungrateful. Their parents may struggle hard to make ends meet so that they can be educated, but once they have become prosperous and successful, they tend to forget their parents. Perhaps one may earn as much as £3 in a month, and then, when his parents ask him for financial help, he may give them a shilling. If they ask him for more three months later, he may reply in such terms as, "Why don't you try to get it out of me by force? Do you think money grows on trees?" Ah, what a wicked child! You had better take care of your parents. Although they may be poor and wretched, you should remember that despite their poverty, they were still able to bring you up. Only after they are dead, will you realize that there is nobody as good as one's parents. Therefore, honour your parents, for they were responsible for bringing you into the world. However brilliant you may be - even if you have doctorate degrees in twelve disciplines, sixteen different legal qualifications, enough mastery of theology to give you title to thirteen bishoprics and can wear twenty clerical stoles all at once, you should never be disrespectful to your father. Model yourself on the many brilliant Nigerians who were educated in England, yet continue to love and cherish the Yoruba Kingdom as their native land. Many of them wear our native attire and love to be photographed in it. Some wear our special traditional robes as a symbol of national identity and as a gesture of respect for the Nigerian culture in which they were brought up. At the same time, they give due respect to their elders. I would also like to remind you young man that charity begins at home, for if you don't respect your own father who is close to you, you can never respect Africa which is your country of origin. In such circumstances, how can you be regarded as good for anything?

'Always exchange ideas with your father, and seek his advice. Then he will come to regard you as an intelligent child. When your parents reprimand you for any misdeed, keep silent, make them see that you regret what you have done, and promise that you will never do it again. Never talk back when you are being reprimanded. Mind you, some children like to argue with their parents, and this is especially common among girls in their dealings with their mothers; the parent has only to utter a word, and the daughter will use it to launch an endless argument. Other children can become so aggressive that they are tempted to use violence on their mothers. Ah! God is very tolerant; I think if I were God, I would ordain that every hand raised in anger should remain permanently stuck in that position! Although such children are not common, it is certain that if they do not make a timely repentance, they will bring upon themselves divine retribution before they die – which might mean being struck blind. I therefore ask you, young man, would you prefer that? Sometimes your parents may annoy you, but you must be tolerant, and remember that the older they become, the more childishly they behave. However, I appeal to you, please never give your parents cause to curse you, because that can certainly have the most unhappy consequences, especially if the child is at fault.'

"I have said a lot about children in general, but so far nothing about mischievous children – that is, those whose entire deportment and fundamental nature are difficult to the point of being downright evil. I do not propose to devote much time to them now, but I will, nonetheless, tell you a short fable, which I hope you will find entertaining and instructive. This is how it goes.

"Once upon a time a woman gave birth to an exceptionally handsome child, but as soon as he was born he began to address her in these terms: 'Alas! So this is life. Why was I ever born into such a world as this? I didn't realize it would be such a terrible place, I had expected Earth to be as beautiful as Heaven. Alas, look at the contents of the ditches, and the hillocks of animal dung, even at the centre of town! Filth lies everywhere. What sort of mess have I got myself into? I must regretfully announce that I will soon be going back to Heaven.'

"Dear brave hunters, those were the words of the new-born baby. As soon as he had spoken he got up from the spot where he had been born and, giving nobody the chance of picking him up, marched straight into his mother's bedroom, where he took soap and a sponge and bathed himself thoroughly all over. Then he wrapped himself in a piece of cloth and sat himself upright. A little later he went back into the room and ate six corn-meal rolls before coming out, and he would certainly have eaten more if there had been any more, because as soon as he came out, he screamed for more food to the great astonishment of everyone in town.

"Soon news of this strange child got round, and everyone in town came to see him, but he was not pleased to see them. When, on his seventh day, it was time for him to be given a name, his parents prepared a great feast, but as the naming ceremony was about to begin, he himself said: 'My name is Ajantala [Urchin] .'

"Ajantala had been feeling rather irritated ever since preparations for the naming ceremony had begun. After a while, he went to the area where the feast was being prepared and took up the spoon to stir the stew-pot on the fire. This surprised everyone who saw him and they began to repeat the adage, 'Nature is the victim of its own creation, and

Ajantala's mother will most likely fall victim to her own offspring.' "When Ajantala heard this, he picked up a cane and set about thrashing all the people who were preparing the feast, so that they all fled in panic. His anger remaining unabated, he proceeded to where the guests were feasting and thrashed them mercilessly. Both youths and strong full-grown men tried to fend him off, but were unable to resist him. In the end, they all fled with Ajantala in pursuit. The street was in total chaos, with people running for their lives and calling on their gods to rescue them. The Christians were calling on their Saviour, the Moslems were calling on Allah, and the various pagans and animists were calling on whatever gods they believed in. There was a terrible commotion and a very bad occasion for the party guests.

"Once Ajantala had chased them as far as he could, he returned home, still boiling with rage, and hissed, 'If you will not be guided by experience, I will certainly make you learn by experience!' So saying he went into his mother's bedroom, where he smashed six china plates, and when he came out he trampled six hens to death.

"A man who was standing nearby cried, 'Alas! You are a wicked child!' but when Ajantala heard this, he slapped the man six times on the face. They settled to fighting and when another man tried to intervene, Ajantala kicked him six times. "Once he had finished kicking him, Ajantala noticed some people playing Warry, so he abandoned the fight in order to take part. He won six times on the trot, and when his elder brother, who had witnessed all these things, began to exclaim, he had got no further than 'Ah!' when his mouth was torn open by Ajantala so that it extended all the way to the back of his head on both sides. Ajantala had certainly become a serious problem!

"Dear brave men; that was the sort of mischief in which this wicked child engaged for a full month. He held the whole town in terror, and offered a constant threat to the public which no one could handle.

"There was a very experienced witch doctor practising in that town and he had boasted as soon as he heard about Ajantala, that it would be a simple matter for him to deal with. He tried to convince the towns people that Ajantala was a changeling child because his behaviour was typical of the fairy sort, and he promised them that once he had the opportunity to meet him, he could, by his professional skill, bring everything back under control. So, when the proper time arrived, he made the necessary preparations: he put on a pair of traditional baggy trousers, and knotted his charmed loincloth round his waist over them; over that he wore a heavy black robe with matching hat, and packed his magic bag with magical implements and medicinal charms. His kit included among other things, a brass canister, parrot feathers, gourdlets, oblong gourds, cowrie shells, and a string of snake bone beads. Confident in the magical efficacy of such a collection, the witch doctor took his bag to Ajantala's house. He found Ajantala eating, so he greeted him and sat down to talk to his mother. The first thing to cause him concern was the size of Ajantala's meal (which would have been enough for ten), and he was equally concerned to note the size of his own morsel, which would have done for at least six; though in fact, it had been observed that nobody could eat with Ajantala and claim to be satisfied at the end of the meal.

"Inevitably, Ajantala's name came up in the course of conversation, and as soon as he heard it, Ajantala got up and threw a corn-meal roll at the witch doctor, hitting him in the chest; then he picked up his plate of stew and emptied it onto his head. He then rushed up to him, grabbed his robe by the scruff of the neck, seized his magic bag and set about beating him over the head with it until it burst open. While this scuffle was going on, Ajantala wrapped his robe over his head, untied the charmed loincloth from his waist and began to hit him with that as well.

"My dear comrades, when the pain of this became so severe as to be unbearable, the witch doctor screamed out, and as soon as he managed to free himself from his robe, he abandoned it, and fled for his life. Ajantala pursued him as far as his house before he gave up and returned home, leaving him with a badly bruised body clad only in the baggy trousers and quite winded by his experience. When people came to ask him what it had been like, he replied, 'That child is a truly terrible problem. Never in my entire life have I suffered such dreadful things as I suffered today. He ill-treated me in almost every way you could imagine. He beat me within an inch of my life until I was almost sick with the punishment, and threw me about so much I was lucky my head didn't smash against a rock! Altogether, he gave me a very hard time.'

"This account greatly surprised his audience who agreed that it must have been tough, or such a master would never have had to run home. 'Did you not take any magic charms with you?' he was asked.

"The old man replied, 'Charms against what? Can a tuber fibre survive in a fire? You think it's funny, do you? I told you, he beat me repeatedly and seized my garment. He also hit me with my own charmed loincloth – and haven't you noticed my magic bag is missing? He made away with all my belongings, and I am lucky to have escaped because he obviously intended to finish me off.'

"At this, someone in the audience called out, 'Aha! How did he do it? Where's your underwear – did he seize your hat as well?'

"The old man was angry at this and expostulated, 'Please ask me no more stupid questions! When something very valuable has been lost in a fire, do you concern yourself with the fate of some petty item? Can anyone find life in a raging inferno? I told you that he seized all my belongings and here you are, asking about my hat! Do you not imagine he would have taken my trousers if I'd waited any longer? Look and take note: if any one of you sees him and does not take instant flight, that person will be in imminent danger of death. I will personally drive such a person away if he subsequently runs back here because I don't want anyone bringing further trouble to my own place.'

Ajantala and the Medicine-Man

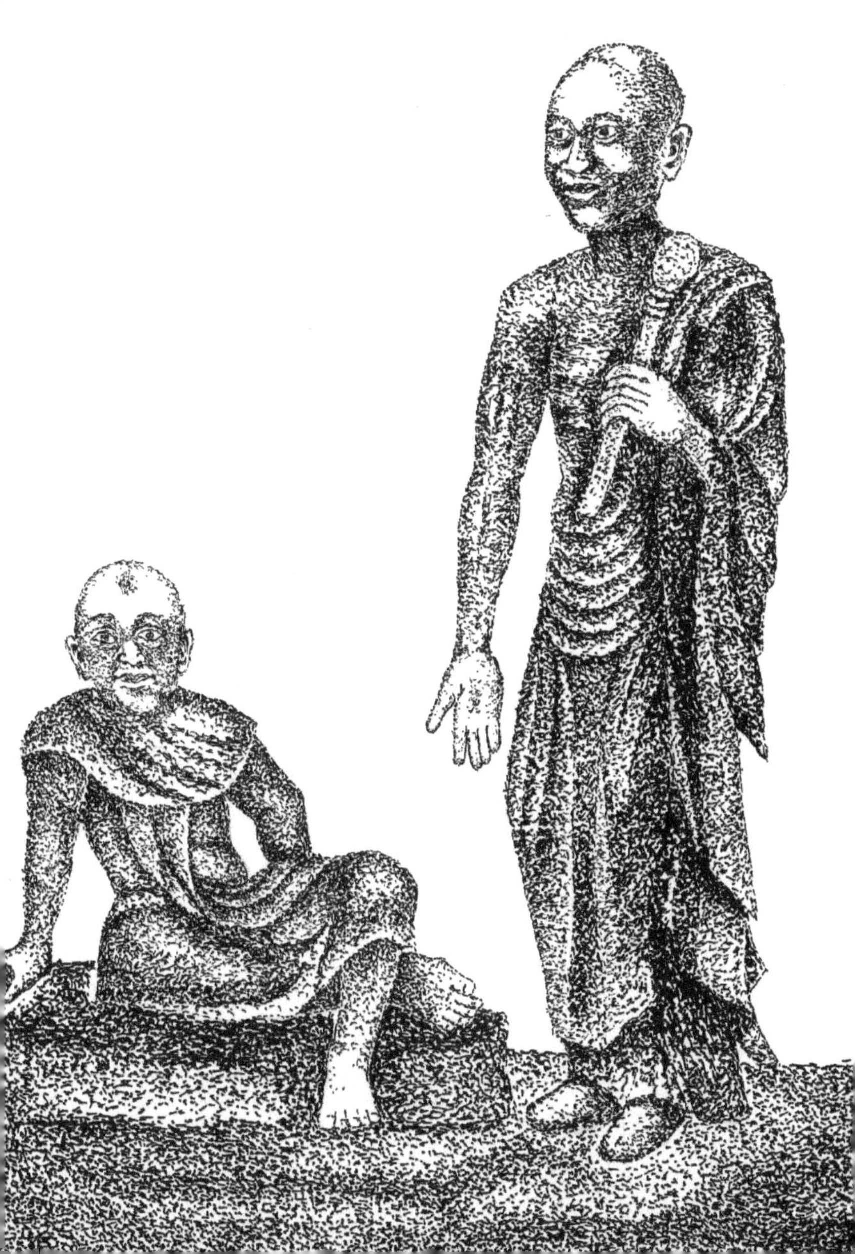

"That was how Ajantala became such a problem at home that eventually his mother could no longer tolerate his nuisance, and took him into a forest where she treacherously abandoned him.

"While Ajantala was wandering about in the forest, he came to a place where he found five animals living together in harmony. They were an elephant, a lion, a tiger, a wolf and a goat. Ajantala pleaded with them to be allowed to join their company as their servant, and they all agreed. "The animals took it in turns to go and look for food every day, while the rest stayed at home. When he returned, the food he had brought would be shared among them. Thus they lived in harmony without quarrels or misunderstandings until this wicked boy came to live with them. As it happened, it was night when he arrived, and it was the goat's turn to look for food next day. Ajantala was ostentatiously well behaved and caused no trouble that night because he was still new to the group. But the following morning, the lion called everyone together and suggested that since they had now acquired a servant, it would be a good idea for the new servant to accompany whoever was due to hunt for food that day. The whole group, including Ajantala, happily fell in with that suggestion, and applauded it.

At first light, the goat prepared himself and set out to hunt for food in the forest, with Ajantula accompanying him as had been suggested. Once they were there, the goat started looking for food but Ajantula just played by himself. The goat made no complaint, feeling that he shouldn't bother him on his first day, taking the view that Ajantula was still new and inexperienced. Nevertheless, once he had found some food and packed it into his bag, the goat asked Ajantula to help him lift it onto his head. But when Ajantula got to him, he seized the goat by the legs and knocked him flat on his back. Before the goat could get up, Ajantula kicked him here and there until the goats face was badly bruised and swollen. The goat cried out for help but there was no one around to rescue him until Ajantula released him. Upon his release, Ajantula warned the goat thus: "If you ever tell anyone at home that I beat you, it will be the worse for you".

After the goat had sufficiently rested for a while, he lifted his load upon his head and set off home with Ajantula following. Just before they arrived at home, Ajantula asked the goat to hand over the load to him and he did. Once they got home and the rest of the animals saw the dishevelled state of the goat, they all made exclamations of dismay and asked him what had happened. But instead of telling the truth, the goat lied as follows: "While I was looking for food, I accidently disturbed a beehive with my head and the bees responded aggressively in defence of their territory by stinging me. But as I ran off I was overwhelmed by a swarm of wasps. That is how my eyelids became swollen and why you cannot see my eyes.

On the following day, it was the wolf's turn to look for food, and Ajantula followed him as before. When the wolf returned home in the evening, his face was swollen and his body was covered in multiple bruises. When the other animals asked him what had happened, he replied "What befell the goat yesterday is exactly what happened to me today, and I have no doubt that the same thing will happen to every one of us". At this point the goat winked at the wolf as best he could with his swollen lids, and they both shook their heads in acknowledgement of a shared secret experience, but Ajantula paid no heed to that.

To cut a long story short, that was how Ajantula mistreated every one of them, including, at last, the Lion. But on the very evening that he had ill-treated the Lion, the five animals held a meeting at which they decided to abandon camp to Ajantula because the trouble he caused was unbearable. The goat suggested that the whole group act quickly and together, leaving the camp the following morning. The animals all agreed and the suggestion was adopted unanimously. They set about packing their belongings, but unfortunately they did not realize that they had played into Ajantala's hand for he had anticipated their plan.

"Once he knew they were all asleep, Ajantala wrapped himself up in leaves and stowed himself in one of the bags, which was easy enough since he was only about eighteen inches in height. Unaware of this latest subterfuge, they all set out early in the morning to look for a new campsite. After they had been walking for a while and covered a considerable distance, the goat started to feel hungry and was tempted to steal some food out of the baggage. He therefore told the rest that he needed to empty his bowels, and they need not wait for him as he would catch them up but that was not true. Once they were out of sight, he started to unpack the baggage, but as he was biting through the bundle in which Ajantala had wrapped himself, Ajantala leapt out and beat him soundly. He knocked him down and kicked him repeatedly. Then he ordered the goat to wrap him in the leaves again and to remain silent, then hand the baggage over to the wolf once they rejoined the group. He hoped that the wolf would be tempted to unwrap him just as the goat had been.

"The goat put the baggage back on his head and hurried to rejoin the group. Once he had caught up with them, they continued on their way together. Shortly thereafter he asked the wolf to relieve him of the load on his head, because he was getting tired. The wolf took the burden, but the same idea soon occurred to him, and he, too, gave the rest of the group the false excuse that he needed to empty his bowels and paid for his subterfuge just as dearly, being beaten up as ruthlessly as the goat had been. Never before had the wolf suffered such a beating; he wanted to scream, but Ajantala held his mouth shut so that he couldn't make a sound, for all that Ajantala was still only a tiny creature. Only after he was tired did he stop beating the wolf and tell him to wrap him up again, and put him back in the baggage. He also ordered him to relinquish the baggage to someone else as soon as he caught up with the group, threatening to beat him again if he failed to calm down quickly. The wolf immediately got his feelings under control, and muttered to himself the adage, 'Whoever thinks he can fool anyone must be prepared for the consequences of such deception.' Thus it was that this mischievous imp beat up everyone, finishing with the elephant. Once Ajantala got hold of him, the elephant fled, trumpeting loudly, but Ajantala ran after him. Soon they caught up with the others, and every one of them ran desperately for his life. The stampede can only be described in one phrase – 'Move or give way' – which each of them expressed in his natural voice. The goat cried 'Meeh!', the wolf howled, the tiger growled, the lion roared and the elephant trumpeted as they all fled in confusion.

"But alas - Ajantala took a different and shorter route to that of the animals that enabled him to wait for them at the other end. Once he had got well ahead, he saw a suitable tree and climbed it, expecting that the animals would want to rest for a while under its shade. Soon they appeared in the distance, strung out one behind the other, and when they reached the tree, they decided to rest just as Ajantala had anticipated, Having been free of Ajantala for some time, none of them realized that he was perched on a branch high above them.

"While they were resting under the tree they began to talk among themselves, making insulting remarks about Ajantala. They described him as a tiny, mischievous creature, totally invulnerable to any form or degree of punishment, however hard one tried to inflict it. 'Is this not an extraordinary form of persecution?' they enquired of each other, 'Only sheer luck can rescue us from this most embarrassing predicament!'

"They directed most of their anger at the goat, blaming him for encouraging them to accept Ajantala into their group when he first appealed to them. Replying to that accusation, the goat exclaimed, 'Ah! But it wasn't me!' At that point, the elephant told the goat to shut up if he didn't want to be trampled to death to which the lion added, 'A welcome idea, just when one is feeling hungry!'

"The goat stood up to swear that if it had been he who had influenced the group to adopt Ajantala, he deserved to be buried alive by supernatural means then and there; but if the allegations against him were untrue, the goat wished that Ajantala should instantly appear by magic to disperse them. After he heard that, Ajantala needed no second bidding and immediately jumped down from the tree, dispersing them in terror.

"Ever since then, the goat has become a domestic animal, the elephant has chosen to live in Africa and India, the tiger and wolf wander in the wilderness and the lion has chosen to live in the veldt. But what became of Ajantala? Did he become a rover of the forest? Certainly not, because God had been observing his activities from the realm of Heaven and seen that his behaviour was totally unacceptable. He therefore ordered that he be brought back to Heaven from whence he had come.

"This story has become common knowledge to such an extent that when people want to describe a wicked or troublesome person, they say, 'He's worse than Ajantala!' That is the end of the story, and I sincerely hope that none of you has such an unpredictable, destructive and maladjusted child to make your life unbearable."

"That was how Iragbeje finished his story and afterwards he addressed us as follows. "Dear brave hunters, no amount of words will fill a bushel, so let us relax and enjoy ourselves for it will be dark soon. Tomorrow we will talk about a different subject altogether."

"After that, we set about enjoying the many varied and delicious dishes that Iragbeje had provided. The people of Mount Langbodo came out to welcome us, and the celebrations continued until nightfall after which we retired to sleep.

CHAPTER 7

The Second Day with Iragbeje in the House of Seven Bedrooms

When we woke up next morning, Iragbeje took us to another room that was twice as beautiful as the one where we had spent the night. Then once we had all settled down, he addressed us as he had the previous day.

"Yesterday I spoke to you about children, but today I will be talking about adults, who can be just as obstinate. Please take note of how I myself would address such people.

"'Well, obstinate man,' I would say, 'have you changed your behaviour? If you have not yet done so, I advise you to do so quickly, because the inevitable fruit of obstinacy is ultimate humiliation. Obstinacy is the worst form of human behaviour, and any adult who is guilty of it exposes himself to humiliation. An obstinate person will exhibit irrational behaviour in pursuit of his obsession; he does the opposite of what is asked, though there is no one forcing him to behave in that way. One of our adages holds that a mature, responsible person will live and act in full understanding of his own means and capabilities; a wise man has no desire for what he cannot obtain, but a stupid man lies under no such constraints, and will foolishly imitate whatever others do, without regard for the limitations imposed by his personal capabilities or resources. Alas, thoughtless man! You have no inkling of what resources your neighbour can command. Be warned! If you take no thought for the fact that you may be living beyond your present means, you will sooner or later come to regret the consequences of your recklessness.

"'I must also advise you that whenever anyone offends you, and then apologizes for his wrongdoing, you should pardon him speedily. Remember that he has asked your forgiveness, not on account of your social status, personal magnetism, wealth or influence, but because he loves you. People respect love even when they have no regard for influence. If you fail to accept his apology at once, you will lose his respect and he may well feel obliged to tell you to please yourself.

"'Once the situation has deteriorated thus far, you will realize that you have no choice but to walk away in shame. Obstinate man! You should remember that you have become notorious for your intractable and stubborn nature, and for as long as you have such qualities, you will forfeit the respect of those who love you, such as your friends and close acquaintances whose good advice you have spurned. They will come to hate you and disregard you completely, deeming you to be a worthless individual. Moreover, if you get into trouble they will offer you no help.'

"Nevertheless, I want you all to realise that there is a difference between obstinacy and a proper steadfast determination. Everyone knows the difference between what is good and what is bad, because such knowledge is among the natural endowments of mankind. Therefore, if you decide to do what is right, even if thousands of people attempt to dissuade you, you should ignore them, and proceed on your chosen course. If you are reviled for it, you should know in your heart that none of the evil names they give you is your true name, because you know within yourself that you are a good man. Moreover, once you are successful, those who criticized you will offer respect and praise. Therefore your life needs to be carefully planned on virtuous lines and with proper forethought. Examine your plan carefully so that you know what is right and do not behave in the manner of an obstinate or disrespectful person.

"I would like to illustrate what I have been saying with a little story, so that you can appreciate the downfall of an obstinate person.

"Once upon a time there was a lion. He lived in an area of forest where there were no other lions, and he felt like eating as and when he pleased, without going to the effort of hunting. So one day he summoned all the animals of the forest together, and addressed them in the following terms:

"'First I must thank you all for honouring my invitation to attend this meeting today, which demonstrates your respect for me as your King. You must also realize that I am no tyrant, even though I have at various times killed some of you for food, although I would like to impress upon you that I didn't do it for pleasure. Nature provides every creature with its own particular food, and we all know that thoughts of hunger override thoughts of friendship. Some of you are happy to graze on vegetation, some of you eat fruits, and it is just as true that others like the wall gecko feed on the carcasses of their fellow animals. As you all know, I am one of the last group, but since I love you, I suggest that you make arrangements among yourselves to come to me voluntarily one at a time, to be killed to feed me. Such an arrangement that thoughts of hunger override thoughts of friendship. Some of you are happy to graze on vegetation, some of you eat will give everyone the opportunity to know beforehand when he is due to die, and whoever's turn it is next, will thus be able to organize the last few days of his life. Furthermore, you all know that I roar whenever I am hungry, and there is no doubt that the sheer volume of my voice must arouse great fear in you all. But if there is an arrangement whereby every one of you knows when it is his turn to die, and voluntarily comes to be killed, there will no longer be any need for me to roar and the rest of you animals can go on enjoying your lives undisturbed. That is the plan which I commend to you.'

"Once the lion had finished this address, an uneasy silence descended upon the assembly that ended when a wolf rose to reply. 'Greetings, comrades,' he began. 'I draw your attention to one of the statements made by the King. He mentioned the various sorts of food which every animal eats that I think was the most important element in his address. But I also think that there is an important aspect to be considered when we are making arrangements to go to the King one by one, and that is, that not all the animals of the forest should be asked to go. For example, I don't think animals such as myself eat any less meat than the King does because I eat both wild and domestic animals – indeed, I don't know how it would feel not to eat a lamb every day. Therefore, I think that if one third of the animals come to me, while the rest go to the King to be killed, the idea would be so admired that it would bring the King everlasting fame throughout the forest. This is my suggested modification to the King's proposal.'

"Next the tiger got up to speak. 'Your Kingly majesty, your suggestion was clear enough, and what our honourable friend the wolf said was equally important. But a point I would like the assembly to note is that if we were to fall in with the wolf's idea, there might soon be no animals left for the King. Therefore, if one third of the animals should go to the wolf, I think it would be reasonable for half to come to me. In this connection, I hasten to say that when it comes to a question of hunting animals for food, the wolf is not as proficient as I, and if it comes to speed, few animals can out-run me. "'Should beauty be a consideration, then you can see for yourself that with I my black and orange striped fur, am very well endowed in that respect. Apart from our honourable friends the deer and the antelope, very few can match my loveliness! As for the capacity to arouse

Lion called a conference of Animals and asked
them to come to him one by one to be devoured
and so save them the agony of hearing him roar
whenever he was hungry.

fear, the only advantage that the King has over myself is his possession of the crown that is his symbol of authority. No lesser animal has ever dared to look on me for long, for it is forbidden. When it comes to the consumption of domesticated animals, I can eat a whole cow without feeling that I've eaten very much at all, and see no need to bother with a mere lamb. Therefore, my suggestion is that all the important personalities among us should be exempt from coming to the King for slaughter. I include the honourable elephant, that formidable lord of the jungle, who is also a distinguished personality in his own right, and myself, the honourable tiger, the prince of the jungle, whose presence evokes such fear in the minds of the lesser animals. The honourable wolf may be exempt as well because he is fourth in command to the King. Apart from those three, all the rest of the animals should have to go to the King for slaughter. I think we should appoint the fox to compile a list of the animals to come forward, so that each will know when his turn has come. I have no doubt that the fox will organize this properly for he is very clever, and I thank this assembly for giving attention to these proposals.'

"After the tiger had finished speaking the elephant supported him, and the rest of the animals agreed.

"The fox when compiling the list, placed his own name first. Thus he should have been slaughtered on the morning of the second day after the meeting - but he failed to show up. He put in no appearance in the afternoon or the evening either, so on the following morning the lion sent for the elephant, the tiger and the wolf and told them how the fox had missed his appointment, despite his name being first on the list. That surprised the other three and they sent for the fox immediately.

"Soon he arrived, and they asked him why he had behaved so disrespectfully. They had hardly finished when the fox began to narrate his story, as follows.

"'May you live long and reign as the King of the animals! I pray that you will never fall victim to an enemy, or fall into any trap. May God also continue to guide and protect you in all events. I am sure that if you did not love and trust me, you would never have delegated to me the responsibility for compiling the list, for who am I among the rest of the animals? I was most surprised when my name was mentioned at the meeting in connection with preparing the list of names, and I pray that the love which you bear for me should never fade away. Far from it, I hope that it will continue to thrive perpetually, so that after I die you will continue to look after my family. Please be assured, I would never dare behave at all disrespectfully towards you, even though it might appear so. Can you see the great mahogany tree over there? (Here he pointed in its direction.) That's where I live. I hope you can also see the big teak tree close to the mahogany? (Once again, he pointed it out.) There are four other animals like yourselves living there: a lion, an elephant, a tiger and a wolf. They have prevented me from coming to you since yesterday, and they are forever terrorizing all the animals who live in that area. If you don't get rid of them, I doubt that any animal will ever come to the King to be slaughtered.'

"This information came as a surprise to all four of the major animals, who had never suspected that there were any to match them in the forest. The lion spoke first. 'Can it really be that there is another lion in the forest?'

"The fox replied, 'Your majesty, it is true.'

"The lion then asked him again, 'But are you sure?'

"'I am absolutely sure,' the fox said, 'but my own observation is that although your counterparts are about the same size as your good selves, they are not as strong as you are, because although they have all pursued me on several occasions, none has succeeded in catching me. I have no doubt that if you fight with them, you will overpower them and kill them, and once this has been accomplished, meat for the King will be plentiful and regular.'

"Nothing in the fox's presentation, especially his tone of voice, suggested to the listening animals that he was lying to them. They therefore decided to follow him to where he said their rivals were to be found, and meet them in person.

"The fox led them to a deep well, which was very full. When they got there, he pointed down the well and asked them to look, for there they would see the animals he was talking about. When the four looked into the well, they saw their own reflections in the water. They snarled at their own reflected images, and lashed their tails at what they saw – which was, of course, their own reflected actions. In the end, they decided to challenge the images and jumped into the well where they drowned. That was the end of their story, but only the lion had been destined to drown himself as he had allowed himself to be carried away by his own stubborn ambition when he first summoned the other animals to come to him. I ask you! Who ever heard of such a request before?

"I have told you the story of one obstinate individual, but I want to tell you the story of another such individual as follows:

"A certain man died, and left his son one hundred pounds. The son spent all the money on consumer goods of the most fragile kind, such as demijohns, tumblers, bottles of various sorts, mirrors, dinner plates and the like, which he acquired as opening stock for a new business. One morning he arranged all these articles, one on top of the other, and as he contemplated the beauty of this arrangement, he was so pleased that he muttered the following words to himself.

"'The one hundred pounds which I inherited was certainly a lot of money, as it was the same amount which I used to purchase all these articles. If I sell them I will surely make a further £100 in profit, and my assets will then amount to two hundred. That is surely a very large sum, and if I use it to acquire more merchandise, will my profit not grow to four hundred? Surely, I will be well off indeed with four hundred pounds! That is how people get rich quick! Again, if I invest it in my business, I am bound to realize another four hundred pounds in profit, and I will then have eight hundred pounds in assets, which will put me on top of the world, an object of universal adoration!

"'But still, even that that eight hundred pounds should not lie idle. If I plough that back into my business as well, it should yield a substantial profit, which could bring my net worth up to two thousand. Once I can achieve that sum, I will be famous throughout the country, and wield an influence which none will dare to challenge. Nevertheless, even having so much money, I will continue to invest it in my business, until the two thousand grows to four thousand, and that to eight thousand until I eventually become a millionaire. Only when I am a millionaire will I indulge myself with material luxuries of all sorts, and the adoration of the people. Even so, the more one speculates, the more one accumulates. I will carry on speculating with my money, and if I continue to apply the profit to buying more merchandise, my assets will grow to about a billion. Only then will I relax and get married, but who in this country will be my bride? A princess, I think!

"'After we are married, and she has come to live with me, I will begin to behave arrogantly towards her, for she will be my wife whom I have married as one of the privileges which my financial status commands. She may be a princess, but I will be entirely independent of her father's financial resources. Sometimes, when she has prepared my food, I will refuse to eat it. This will certainly make her unhappy so she will send for her mother to plead with me on her behalf. Even when they both kneel down before me, I will ignore them which will deeply distress my wife who will clasp my leg, saying, "Please look at me, my darling. You must realize that I love you, and would never let you go hungry without good reason. Your food was late today because the firewood which I used for cooking was drenched in the rain that fell yesterday that prevented it burning properly. I appeal to you, therefore, please forgive me for my mother's sake, and I will never let this happen again. Rather than let you starve, I will go in search of dry firewood wherever I can find it." Naturally, I will feel compassion for my wife, but nonetheless, I will choose to exercise the privilege conferred by my financial status by giving her a gentle kick, like this –'

"By now the man was completely oblivious to his surroundings, muttering to himself and absorbed in his daydreaming. As he muttered that last phrase 'like this' - he gave a kick - and all the fragile merchandise he had purchased with his £100 smashed to pieces! When the vapour of a dream evaporates, then reality will dawn. It was too late for this man to return to his senses; an obstinate dreamer, he had anticipated kicking a princess when he was still far from well off and thought of performing wonders once he was a rich man.

"My dear friends, my next topic will be regret and kindness. I will only say a little about this topic, before going on to illustrate it with a story.

"Regret is a blemish on the human soul, and one which can never be completely eradicated. If there were no such thing as regret, life on Earth would be almost as pleasant as life in Heaven. That's why the elders are so fond of quoting the proverb:

For all sad words of tongue and pen

The saddest are these: "It might have been!"

But remorse for what has been done is futile – you'll excuse me for quoting a parable.

"With regard to kindness, it is true that one should be kind on principle, but one should nevertheless know whether kindness is appropriate and the sort of person most likely to benefit from it. Some people may decide to be kind for no definite reason, just because it pleases them to be kind. They give no thought to whether their acts of kindness are morally justified or socially desirable. Anyone who is inappropriately generous will do more harm than good. For example, a physically healthy man who begs for alms should never be given any. Alms should be given only to those who are physically unable to provide for themselves, however hard they try, such as the elderly and infirm, or those who are helpless by reason of physical handicap. Listen to this story which I will tell you, for I want you to learn a lesson from it.

"Once upon a time there was a man who went travelling abroad, and one day, as he approached a town, he found a tiger in a metal cage. The cage was, in fact, a trap which the townspeople had set for the tiger that had been terrorizing them. The cage was so constructed that once the tiger was inside, it would be impossible for him to leave it without assistance from outside.

"When the tiger saw the traveller, he begged him to release him from the cage, but the man refused. The tiger pleaded with him time and time again, but he still refused. In the end the tiger lamented, 'Alas! What have I done to deserve such treatment? Do you live only in the present, giving no thought for the future? It is true that people describe me as a wicked animal, but I know that I am a kind animal. Surely you realize that people gossip a lot, and that they are equally capable of passing on criticism as well as praise. If you could spare the time to live with me for three days, you would soon conclude that there is no one you would more happily live with than me, the honourable prince of the jungle, as well as a most formidable creature. If you pass on your way and leave me here, some kind person will eventually rescue me from this predicament, and then should I ever see you again, it will be very difficult for you to escape. I am quite sure we will meet again - once I am released.

"When the man had heard all this, he replied, 'You are surely right and I understand you well. The man who takes proper precautions is safe from danger whatever his personal bravery may be, and excessive precautions never do any harm. But if I were to set you free, how would I know that you would not immediately pounce upon me and tear me to pieces?'

"The tiger replied, 'If that is your principal concern, please do not worry. I promise that if you set me free, I will never do you harm' Please hurry up and open the door as time is running out.

"The man was so carried away by the tiger's impressive appearance of sincerity that he forgot that the tiger had made it only under the force of the life-threatening circumstances in which he currently found himself. He therefore opened the cage, but as soon as the tiger got out, he pounced on the man intending to kill him. However, the man earnestly pleaded with him to spare his life, and suggested that they should present their cases to a panel of the first five creatures that they met, and both should agree to be bound by their decisions. The tiger agreed, and they continued on their way, both trusting in this agreement.

"Soon they met a goat, and the man immediately told it the story of how; while he was passing, he had seen the tiger trapped in the metal cage, how he had refused to help when the tiger first entreated him, but how the tiger's repeated blandishments had aroused his compassion and so he had set him free. He went on to say how surprised he had been when the tiger attempted to kill him despite his kindness..

"Once he had heard the case in full the goat said, 'Human beings are useless parasites and notorious for character-assassination. Since I have been with my owner, he has never allowed me any peace. He gives me no care when I bear my babies, but once, after a hard struggle, I have brought them up on my own, he comes to deprive me of them and sell them, devoting the proceeds entirely to his own selfish ends. Once he has given me some bananas in the morning, he leaves me to forage on leaves for the rest of the day. He never gives me any of his yams or maize to eat, and once he has eaten his own meal he beats me almost to death. It follows that all human beings are wicked, and the tiger should certainly kill you.'

"Once the goat had finished delivering his judgement, the tiger pounced on the man intending to kill him, but he quickly reminded the tiger that according to their agreement they had still to seek opinions from four more creatures, so they continued on their way. Soon they met a horse, and the man stopped to present his case while the tiger stood to one side and listened. The horse, giving his judgement, began, 'Human beings speak with the Cross on their breasts and the Devil in their hearts. What you have just reported may well be true, but there is more bad than good in human nature; goodness is scarce, and you will try many times before you meet a good man! Men and animals both know well enough how patient I am, but humans exploit and abuse my patient nature. They mount my back all the time, expecting me to carry them about, but if I am tired and can only plod, they kick me and whip me to force me to run. Sometimes, if this punishment becomes unbearable, I lose my temper and throw them from my back. When that happens, they then complain that a horse has thrown them off! Ah, what a wonderful people! The tiger should definitely kill you.' "At this point the tiger once again pounced on the man to kill him, but he reminded him that they still had three more creatures to see.

"Soon afterwards they arrived at an orange tree, and the man presented his case. When he had finished the orange tree began his judgement as follows. 'You have given a reasonable report, but I am sorry to say that I can never back any human being, because they are useless. You can see that I stay in the same spot all the time, and offer harm to no one. People come to relax and enjoy themselves under my shade in the hot dry season. When my fruits are ripe, instead of climbing me with care to pluck them for food, people throw stones at me so that most of my leaves fall off and my bark is left damaged and exposed. Your wickedness is worse than that of the monkeys, so the tiger should definitely kill you.' "Once the tree had finished its judgement, it took great effort by the man to restrain the tiger from killing him, but they continued their journey and after a short distance, met a dog.

"The man presented his case, but the dog condemned human beings no less than the others, and gave a similar judgement. After that, they had only one more creature to see, but not long afterwards they met a fox.

"Once again the man presented his case, with tears in his eyes, as follows. 'Greetings, fox, I know that you are an honest animal. Please, in God's name, I would like you to give me your honest opinion on this matter. While I was travelling abroad on my own, I saw a tiger in a metal cage as I approached a town. When I first saw him, my immediate reaction was to ignore him completely and continue on my way, but he drew himself to my attention and appealed to me to set him free. At first I refused, on the grounds that he might kill me once I released him. It was as if I knew what was going to happen, for ever since then he has detained me, and now only God can free me from this unfortunate predicament. Nevertheless, the tiger persisted in his appeals to be released, and promised that he would not kill me, so I reconsidered my decision and released him. As soon as I had done so, he pounced on me, and was going to kill me, except that I suggested that we should seek the opinions of other creatures in this connection, and this is why we are here. Therefore, I appeal to you to save me from this predicament, and pray that you will never regret your kindness.'

"Once the man had finished, the fox glared at him unpleasantly, and said, 'Is this your idea of how to present a case? I can't make head or tail of what you're trying to say. Don't you realize that you're standing in the presence of the honourable tiger? Have you no respect for the prince of the jungle, that most formidable creature? If you want me to consider your case at all, you must take your time and present it in proper sequence from the beginning. Moreover, you should narrate it with proper respect, seeing that we are both in the presence of the Master.' So the man began to tell his story all over again, but as soon as he had got to the point where he mentioned having seen the metal cage, the fox interrupted him: 'I beg your pardon, but please, what is "a metal cage"? The man replied, 'It is a cage, made out of metal.' The fox appeared dissatisfied with this, and asked again, 'What did you say "a metal cage" was?'

"At this point the man said, 'Dear fox, I know you are an intelligent animal, so you must surely know what a metal cage is. You certainly know what a fowl-cage is, because fowl are your favourite food. Incidentally, just before this incident took place, I had acquired two or three fowl, which I had intended to present to you on account of your illustrious reputation, which I had often heard praised by the other animals. They are also fond of saying what a kind animal you are. I have not departed from this intention, but now the situation depends on the tiger. However, should I live beyond today you will most certainly have fowl to eat – hen or cock, whatever is your preference, you shall have, for they are all at my disposal.

"'But to return to the point you have raised, there isn't much difference between a metal cage and a fowl-cage except that a metal cage is made of metal and bigger than a fowl cage. I hope that now you understand what this means, and I appeal to you to pass a favourable judgement on me, and may God bless you.'

"Once again the fox reproved the man, saying, 'My dear fellow, do you think of me as "Mr Fox, the fowl-monger"? You are a useless, stupid and irresponsible individual and unless you take me to this metal cage right away, I won't let you go because you will have been proved a liar.' "The fox then turned to the tiger, and said, 'Your worship, whoever thinks he can fool others is only trying to fool himself, and the man who thinks he can fool you is also trying to fool himself. Moreover, any animal of the forest that holds you in no regard is also a fool. Therefore, I appeal to you, at your own discretion, to follow us to the metal cage. I want to deal with this man severely, and when I have given my judgement, it will be my privilege to witness his death.'

"This speech pleased the tiger, who said, 'Dear fox, your summary is perceptive. So carry on, and I will follow you.' Thus the three of them set off together towards the metal cage.

"Once they got there, the fox turned to the man and said, 'Where were you standing?'

"The man pointed the place out with his finger, and said, 'There.'

"'Alright, stand there and let me see you.'

"The man took up his position, after which the fox turned to the tiger, and said, 'Where were you standing, sir?'

"The tiger indicated the metal cage and said, 'Over there.'

"The fox then said, 'Sir, I want you to understand that I am not very bright and it takes me a long time to understand things. Unless you stand where you were at the time, I won't understand what you mean.'

"So the tiger went into the metal cage. At this the fox said, 'Now I'm beginning to understand.' Then he turned to the man and said, 'You liar! I thought you said that you let him out? Why couldn't he come out on his own since the door of the metal cage was left open?'

"The man said, ' It was shut at the time.'

"'How?'

"The man went to shut the door of the cage, and said, 'Like this!'

"The fox asked again, 'Do you reckon that's secure and the tiger can't get out again?'

"The man went to shake the door to make sure it was properly shut. Then he said, 'The tiger cannot get out.'

"At this the fox took a good look at the tiger, after which he burst out laughing, and said, 'Well, tiger, you've been caught, and there you will stay for as long as it takes. You're an ungrateful beast and God will surely punish anyone who turns you loose! As for you, my dear fellow, you can continue on your journey now, but don't forget the fowl that you promised me. I have rescued you from one danger, and may God steer you away from further dangers. I also pray that God may protect you from further mishap. When you get to the town centre, tell the people that the tiger which had been terrorizing them has been caught in a cage, and they should come with their guns, and with bows and quivers full of arrows to punish the ungrateful creature.'

"Thus was the tiger recaptured and dealt with. He pined away for a considerable time, but he realized he was helpless. Both the fox and the man laughed well at his expense. The tiger was humiliated and insulted while all he could do was stand there blinking helplessly. Meanwhile, the man did precisely as the fox had advised, and before long the townspeople came to kill him. As he lay dying, he said to himself, 'Alas, that this should be my final fate! If I had made proper use of the first opportunity that God gave me he would not have withdrawn it and left me to die.'

"Thus did the tiger regret his mistake, but it was too late. It is true that he repented, but only when it was too late to avoid the consequences of his ungrateful behaviour. I pray that none of us ever fall victim to misfortunes of our own making, which we regret too late.

"I have already spoken about acts of kindness and the sort of people whom one should be kind to, but I would like to add something to that. There are certain charitable organizations that are inspired by love of their country and fellow men. They are committed to improving the lot of their country and its people by all available means. But these organizations have extensive financial commitments and so run into trouble from time to time. So let me make this clear to you, they need your financial and moral support. Therefore whatever amount you can spare, be it a halfpenny, a penny or a pound, give it to help them. Money devoted to a good cause is money well spent, and God will reward you with good health.

"There are also gifted children who although brilliant, lack sufficient financial means to pursue their education to the limit of their abilities; likewise, there are other young people who never get the opportunity to realize their full potential. These are children whom wealthy people should endeavour to help financially.

"Well, my dear friends, I think I have said enough for today, and now I should stop so that we can spend the rest of the day enjoying ourselves."

When he had finished talking, we relaxed and enjoyed ourselves until nightfall. We still had five more days to spend with Iragbeje. But I won't mention the strange things which we saw and heard during those five days, because time is running out. Instead I will tell you what we experienced on the seventh day.

CHAPTER 8

The Seventh Day with Iragbeje in the House of Seven Bedrooms, and the Departure from Mount Langbodo

After breakfast on the seventh day, Iragbeje took us on a tour of the town of Mount Langbodo. We devoted some time to that before we returned to the house for lunch, after which we played games, entertaining ourselves with racing, wrestling, jumping, somersaulting, climbing trees and many other physical pursuits. Once the fun was over, Iragbeje took us to the last room, which we had not seen so far, though we had been in the other six rooms during our six days in the house.

This seventh room was quite unlike those we had seen before, as everything – ceiling, floor, walls and furnishings – was absolutely white as snow. When we entered, Iragbeje made us line up before him, and warned us not to sit down. He himself was wearing white robes, and began by addressing us as follows.

"We have talked about many things since you arrived here, but today we will talk about our Creator. My dear friends, because you are strong, brave, diligent men, resolute in your determination to be of service to your country, I want you to realize from the outset that whatever is begun in God's name will never end badly, and that is an indisputable fact. God is great; God is omnipotent, our Creator, the King of Heaven, immortal and invisible, almighty, holy, omniscient and omnipresent. I want you people who have come to Mount Langbodo to listen attentively to a short story which I will tell you, and which illustrates the greatness of God.

"Once upon a time there was a king who was very great, rich, and blessed with children. His kingdom was greater than any neighbouring kingdom, and he himself was very handsome, but his conduct was bad. He was as wicked as the Devil, crueller than a monkey, and a danger to all whom he encountered; moreover, he habitually exhibited a demeanour of embittered melancholy.

"This king was unaware that the manner makes the man and that nothing can be more pleasant than a cheerful countenance; though despite his intrinsic wickedness, he was a regular attender at church. Thus it was one day while the choristers were singing and the organist was displaying his best skills, the king noticed that one hymn sounded more beautiful than any of the others. Since it was sung in a foreign language he didn't understand, he asked for the words to be translated. The king was told that they meant, 'He has brought down the powerful from their thrones, and has lifted up the lowly.'

"My dear friends, I must tell you that at this the king was deeply offended. He began to sweat profusely, and his eyes grew red with rage. Had it been practicable at that moment, he would have shot the organist and beheaded the choristers, but instead he turned to a nearby courtier and said, 'After the service, please remind me to teach these ignorant people some lessons. Now I understand why they always conduct the service in a foreign tongue that I don't understand. I realize now it is so that they can insult me with impunity. But I intend to impress upon them that I am famous all over the world. No king can afford to deny knowing me, neither can any chief dare disregard me, for if God has his throne in Heaven, then I have mine on Earth. If I can't remove Him from his heavenly throne, I'm just as certain that He can't remove me from mine!'

"Thus spoke the king, from the midst of his comfortable life. He was setting himself up in competition with God, and had forgotten that He was his Creator. But God was watching him from Heaven. God smiled, and said to one of His angels who was standing nearby, 'Learn a lesson from this – didn't you hear what that ignorant king said? He has forgotten all about Me because he has an easy life. I often notice that people are rude to Me, but instead of becoming angry and punishing them severely I feel sorry for them, because I know that they are My creatures. But what can one say of one who speaks thus? I know that I created him, and if I felt I must respond in the same manner as he has behaved towards Me, could I not punish him just as I like? For example, I could turn him into an animal, or a wild plant; or I could turn him into a chimaera, half man, half beast; or I could inflict on him some really unusual punishment, just to make him realize that I am his Creator. Nevertheless, I will not actually do any of these things to him; instead, I want you to go to Earth immediately and take his place. Do not lay hands on him, but give him the opportunity to repent. Only when he has repented may you reinstate him.'

"The angel immediately did as God instructed leaving Heaven for Earth. Only seconds after the king had finished speaking, the angel cast him into a hypnotic trance. Then he turned the king's clothes into rags and his gold necklace into brass. The angel then took on the identical appearance of the king so that no one would notice the least difference. While this was happening, the king remained in a trance and when the service was over, everyone else went home. The sexton shut the church doors, and the angel went back to the palace to discharge the duties of the displaced king.

"At midnight, the king woke up in the church. He looked about, confused as to where he was, and started to look for a way out. As he picked his way through the darkness, he stumbled over the pews and blundered into the organ. He was quite confused by the darkness which disoriented him so that he could recognize nothing. At last he found the door, and banged on it with all his strength. When the sexton heard the noise he immediately came to investigate, but no one could have expected what he saw when he opened the door. A man clad only in rags and tatters rushed out at him, so the sexton ran away, thinking it must be a lunatic. "The ex-king was surprised at his reaction, but he was still in a confused state as he set out for the palace. Once he got there, he found the gates locked with the security guards sleeping beside them (the new king being well inside the palace). So he banged on the gates with his fist and shouted, 'Open the gates to me!'

"The security guards woke up, and asked, 'Who are you?'

"He replied, 'It is I, the king.'

"When they heard this they burst out laughing, and said, 'You're a good-for-nothing drunkard.'

"This annoyed him, so that he shouted, 'Who do you think you're talking to? You'll all regret those words in the morning!'

"He went on trying to impress them, but everything he said seemed funny to them, until at last one of the guards opened the gates to see who was pestering them. He took one look and shut them quick, saying to the others, 'This is a pathological maniac, and you'll be in danger if you go out,' so, to cut a long story short, there he stayed until morning.

"In the morning, when the gates were opened, he went into the palace compound, but he hadn't gone far when he was arrested as a lunatic and taken before the king (which is to say, the angel). When the angel saw him he felt compassion for him, and ordered that he be given new clothes. He told the courtiers that the man was not a lunatic, but a clown, and appointed him court jester, with the use of a house in the palace. Nevertheless, the king still found the whole situation very confusing. 'Is this a dream or real life?' he asked himself. 'If I was once a king, how do I now come to be a comedian? I don't understand this at all.'

"Time passed quickly, and a year later the real king had hardly changed at all except to become more despondent and morose. Then one day, he finally realized the nature of his mistake and recalled his foolish remarks made a year ago and then became very frightened of God. It was on a Saturday that he repented, and he went straight to church first thing on Sunday morning, before the church bell had even started tolling. Once he was there, he knelt down to offer a short prayer for his sins to be forgiven, and when the service began he paid more attention to the words of the song. "Once again they reached the line, 'He has brought down the powerful from their thrones, and has lifted up the lowly', which he sang with all his might and with strongest emphasis. My dear friends, I may say in this connection that the real king had a powerful voice that was slightly out of tune so that when the congregation laughed at him, he took no notice, but muttered to himself, 'You can roll around with laughter if you like, but I know what I'm doing. You're laughing at me now because I raised my voice, but a time will come when it shall be my pleasure to roar before you.'

"Soon the service came to an end. Everyone else went home but the real king stayed behind. Once the congregation had gone, he went to the altar where he knelt down on hands and knees to pray seriously to God before he, too went home. Shortly after he arrived home, he received a summons to appear before the king (i.e. angel). When he arrived, the angel dismissed everyone else. Once they had all left, the angel rose from his throne and shut all the doors and windows so that the room was in complete darkness. In such a situation, it is the patient man who gets what he wishes. So the ex-king stood in the dark, waiting for whatever might happen. Soon he heard the sound of heavy footsteps going through the house, loud enough for the pounding of a thousand people. The walls and floor began to shake, and a gust of wind blew shrill throughout the building. All these signs indicated that the angel was about to reveal his identity as the envoy of the Almighty. After this, silence descended, and a great light shone throughout the house. This was because the angel had shed his earthly identity as a king, and revealed his true form as the envoy of God. The man looked up and saw that his robes were as white as snow and his eyes clear as crystal. His skin was fresh as a baby's and his shoes shone like polished brass. The man was very frightened and threw himself to the ground where he covered his face with his hands. Presently the angel began to address him, as follows.

"'I am one of the seven angels who attend to God. When you were living a comfortable life, and had forgotten all about your Creator, did you imagine he was not watching you? There is nothing on Earth or in Heaven of which God is without knowledge, for he created it all. You were behaving so foolishly and talking so arrogantly, that you angered God. He asked me to take your place you and not to kill you, but to reinstate you if you repented. You have done that today. Now that you have remembered your Creator, he is no longer angry with you, because he is a merciful God. I command you, therefore, in the name of Almighty God, to rise and resume your authority and throne, and reign over your kingdom. If you use this opportunity wisely, your reign will be long; but if you misuse the opportunity, then God will strip you of your dominion.'

"As soon as the angel had finished speaking, he returned to his home in Heaven, and the king found himself back on his throne once more, and in great fear of God.

"So ends my story, my dear friends, visitors to Mount Langbodo. Nevertheless, I would like to impress upon you that every man should praise the bridge that carries him over, and it would be unkind for anyone to bite the hand that feeds him, for one good turn deserves another. Anyone who fails to appreciate an act of kindness throws away the chance of future benefits; therefore, if we are prosperous and comfortable in our lives, we should remember God with gratitude." When Iragbeje had finished his story, he asked us to start packing, and prepare to return to the palace, because the following day we would be leaving Mount Langbodo to return to our own country. We therefore set about packing, and once that was complete, we left at about seven o'clock in the evening of our seventh day in Iragbeje's House of Seven Bedrooms, to return to the palace of the Mount Langbodo.

Once we were there, we sent a message to inform the King of Mount Langbodo of our arrival. He ordered that we be taken to his chambers of state that had been illuminated with various lights and were bright as day. There he received us at exactly eight o'clock, and after greeting us, he gave us the following gifts to present to our own king: six diamond rings, six gold necklaces, six beaded crowns, six beaded sceptres, six leather cushions, six household ornaments and six copies of the Holy Bible in six different languages. He also gave us a letter to bear to our King, written and illuminated in gold and silver inks. It read as follows:

The Palace,
Mount Langbodo,
July 22nd, 1933

To the King of the country of the following brave hunters:
Kako, Imodoye, Akara-Ogun, Olohun-Iyo, Elegbede-Ode, Efoiye, and Aramada-Okunrin

Your Royal Highness,
Your ambassadors arrived here safely, and I was happy to see them. I am sending these small

gifts in sets of six according to the ancient Yoruba custom which, I hasten to assure you, is still sometimes observed even now. I offer you six of each of these articles as a symbolic gesture, mindful of the traditional meaning attached to the number six, standing as it does for an emblem of the initiation of friendship and a pledge of peaceful intentions. In addition, I offer the advice that the best progress of your country is that you should encourage your people to love one another so as to develop a spirit of moral awareness; for where there is an active conscience and shame for misdeeds, there may in time be virtue. If your people possess a conscience, they will not steal from each other, nor will they indulge in malicious or untruthful gossip, neither will they be disobedient or arrogant. The young will respect and honour their elders, their elders will nurture the young, and there will be cordial relations between the generations. Moreover, as they love God, so will they also love you, their King.

Please pass on my best regards to your people.

Yours sincerely,
The King of Mount Langbodo

That night, we slept in the palace, and next morning the King gave every one of us many gifts before we left for home. Unfortunately I can't tell you of our experiences on the return journey, for that would take a long time and I do not want to over-burden you with my story.

I have no doubt you will be sorry to learn that not everyone who left Mount Langbodo returned home. How did this come about? In fact, the downfall of most was brought about by arrogance, pure and simple. An arrogant man is the stupidest person in the world, because he thinks that the only way he can obtain the respect of the people is by arrogant behaviour, yet he doesn't realize that it is then that he is most likely to suffer humiliation; and humiliation will certainly attend him sooner or later. If arrogance permeates a household, that household will soon disintegrate; if an entire country is arrogant, it will bring upon itself the wrath of God; if the leading citizens of a country, or a powerful government are arrogant, they will soon be brought down in humiliation. Hence, when most of the delegates to Mount

Langbodo became arrogant, they ceased to listen to each other's advice. There was no more unity or cooperation among them, and everyone behaved to please himself. Yet God applies his own principles, which allow of just two ways of dealing with sinners: either he punishes sinners immediately, or he enters their sins in his record book. On this occasion, punishment was immediate.

When we reached the River of Blood, we found some elves enjoying themselves, for that was the very day when Neptune, who is God of the Sea, was celebrating his annual festival. At that point Kako decided to go and play with the elves, and though we warned him against this foolhardy idea, he paid no heed. After a while, the elves dived down to the bed of the River of Blood and Kako dived down with them. We have heard no news of him since then.

Efoiye and Elegbede-Ode told us they were going to hunt in the forest, but unfortunately they were turned into elves there, and we have seen nothing of them since either. Finally, when we met the Seven Vixen Women, Aramada-Okunrin decided to stay with them, and refused to come back with us. Nevertheless, Imodoye, Olohun-iyo and I certainly got home in good condition, for which we thanked God.

Once we got back, we found that most of the people we had left behind had died while those who were still alive didn't recognize us because we had been away for so long. When we went to see the King, we found that he had aged considerably; his eyesight had grown weak, and he couldn't recognize us at first, but when we presented him with the gifts and the letter from the King of Mount Langbodo, he remembered who we were, and was very happy to embrace us. He gave us a warm welcome and presented us with many gifts, from which we became wealthy ever after. Thus ends the story of my journey to Mount Langbodo.

Three members of the delegate of Brave Hunters that made a successful journey to Mount Langbodo and returned home

My dear friends, that is my message to the world for now, and I hope you will have learnt a profitable lesson from the experiences of my life. Goodbye! I am going home now. As soon as he had finished his story, he vanished from sight, but on the floor we found a card bearing the legend:

Akara-Ogun

The Great Illusionist

Ladies and gentlemen of the Yoruba lands, the wisdom of the enlightened teaches us that the experience of our elders, gained over time at the cost of much wear and tear, makes them the wisest of our citizens. I therefore hope you will learn a valuable lesson from the stories in this book. I would also like to remind you that every one of you will go through a difficult phase at some time in his life, and every one of you will have to make his personal journey to his own Mount Langbodo. Every one of you has his own particular problems to overcome, for life consists of a cycle, in which good periods alternate with bad, and they may change from moment to moment. The wheel turns, and no one can control how it affects the events in his life. Therefore, as you pass through your own good and bad times, you should be prepared to accept every situation as it comes, cheerfully and courageously, and remember that Heaven helps only those who help themselves.

So ends my story. Nevertheless, I advise you to be guided by the conventional wisdom, which teaches many things that bring confidence and peace of mind in this world. Don't be seduced by superficial and trifling items, which can only lead to disaster. Goodbye for now, and I hope you will be hearing more from me at some later time. Let me offer a brief prayer for you, before I call for three cheers: may you live long and prosper, and may your nation grow in wisdom and strength; above all, may all the people of Africa continue to advance in all aspects of life, forever and ever.

Hip! Hip! Hip! Hurrah! Hurrah! Hurrah!

Thank you for enjoying this book.

THE END

Acknowledgments

I would like to express my sincere gratitude to the following people who have worked tirelessly with me as a team to assist in the publication of this book: my son, Orileke Mabo, who helped with the Internet problems; the late Chris Gilmore, who edited the manuscript and provided useful pieces of advice, his brother Peter who took over as my editor after Chris's death, Ms Penelope Sowter who typed the manuscript with great care and professionality and, lastly, but not the least, Dr. Ebenezer O Olukoju of the Department of Linguistics and African Languages, University of lbadan, Nigeria, and Dr. Akin Oyetade of the School of Oriental and African Studies, University of London, both of whom helped to read the manuscript and also offered useful pieces of advice.

Edmund Olu Mabo

About the Translator

Edmund Olu Mabo graduated with an Hons degree in product Design and Graphics, an M.A. degree in the same subject, Post Graduate Diploma in Education, Diploma in History of Art and Architecture. He did research in Comparative Education and he is a Fellow of the Royal Society of Arts. He has taught and lectured in art, design and technology for many years in various secondary schools, colleges and higher institutions both in the UK and Nigeria.

He is passionate about drawing, painting and carving and has exhibited his work in Britain, Germany and Nigeria. He also has a passion for African literature, poetry and history. Above all, he enjoys writing and making music. He has illustrated all his written work and undertaken English translations of all five novels of Fagunwa as well as his biography.

Edmund Olu Mabo